Sam's Top Secret Journal

BOOK TWO –
SAM'S SECRET ISLAND

DR. SEAN C. ADELMAN

ISBN: 0615923534

ISBN 13: 9780615923536

Library of Congress Control Number: 2011963659
RaiseExpectations LLC, Seattle, WA

Acknowledgements

This book is again dedicated to all the young families whose hopes and dreams are beginning to blossom.

We have learned that the *Sam* series is a great way to introduce students to inclusion and acceptance.

Thanks to my wonderful family for supporting and inspiring these stories.

Thanks to Dianna Bonder for her wonderful skill at cover art.

I would also like to thank Andrea Hurst and Siri Bardarson for reading/re-reading and editing/improving my original vision.

Table of Contents

From Sam's Top Secret Journal...

Today we're going to Orcas Island for two whole weeks! I love Orcas Island because it always reminds me of camp. Maybe it's because of the big trees and the beaches. Or maybe it's because I get to have fun outdoors all day and I don't have to think about doing homework. Ever!

I can't wait until the ferry ride. Last time we saw some seals swimming nearby. Maybe this time we'll even see a whale. That would be so cool!

Dad is excited because he's going to get to eat his favorite pie at the farmers market we always go to on the island. Dad reallllly likes pie. He even has pie on his birthday instead of cake.

I hope John leaves me alone in the car. Last time we went on a long car ride, he bugged me so much I called him a bad name and I got in trouble.

That was <u>so unfair</u>!

CHAPTER 1

Off to Orcas

Sam's little brother swung his spy periscope towards her, and for the second time in an hour, he almost knocked her journal out of her hands. She slammed the book shut and leaned forward between the driver and front passenger seats.

"John's touching me again!"

"John, keep your hands to yourself," Dad said without taking his eyes off the road.

Sam sat back in her seat.

"Don't let him get to you, Sam," Mom added. "Be the mature one and set an example for your little brother."

Sam slouched down in her seat behind Dad and stewed. Why did she always have to sit by her brother when they rode in the van? Jenny got the whole back seat to herself. Even better, she got to sit with Chestnut, their new Chesapeake Bay Retriever, draped over her lap, and she could stroke her soft fur all she wanted. At sixteen, Jenny was the oldest and spent every car trip with her ear buds practically glued into her ears, her eyes closed, tuning out the rest of the world.

Sam envied her sister's ability to find a quiet place for herself. She didn't have to listen to John shout out "slug bug" every time he saw a Volkswagen beetle on the road or see him making faces at her behind her parents' backs.

Sam opened her journal and began to write about her feelings. Sometimes just the act of writing things down took some of the sting away or helped her think through her problems. Problems like little brothers, learning math, or how to survive seeing her not-so-secret crush, Andrew, at school every day. She was glad she hadn't forgotten to pack the journal, along with a sketchpad and a good supply of colored pencils for drawing. Art had always been one of her biggest passions. Jenny had her music, and Sam had her journal and her drawing.

"I wasn't touching her anyway!" John broke into her thoughts. "I accidentally hit her with my spy periscope while I was trying to see Chestnut in the back seat. That's all."

Sam figured John had "accidentally" hit her with his spy periscope at least a half a dozen times since they'd climbed into the van that morning, but she'd tried her best not to let him make her angry. After all, she was thirteen and almost in eighth grade, and John was nine and still in grade school. Since she was a teenager now and his big sister, she should probably try to act her age.

Sam just wasn't sure how to do that. She knew the condition she was born with, Down syndrome, sometimes created stumbling blocks for her. For example, she enjoyed her math class, but it could be a struggle, and history, which she loved, was full of dates and events that took her longer to memorize than it did for her classmates. Sam had many challenges that most of her friends never had to worry about. Like how to be a good big sister to a little brother who was often smarter than she was, maybe even too smart for his own good. And now Mom and Dad decided they were ready to take on the responsibility of caring for a dog. Sam would be in charge of Chestnut with Jenny gone.

Chestnut was a rescue dog from the local animal shelter, a dog that deserved another chance. They fell in love with her immediately. Her deep brown eyes seemed to promise she was old enough to not chew on Jenny's shoes, Sam's stuffed animals, or John's secret spy gear, while her wagging tail hinted she was young enough to be playful and run after tennis balls and Frisbees in the back yard.

Just then, John swung his periscope around to peer at Chestnut over the back of his seat and Sam barely had time to avoid being bonked in the head. No matter how annoying he got, Sam was determined no one, not even John, would ruin her time on Orcas Island.

The trip to Orcas was different this year. Sam's older sister, Jenny, was going to be a counselor at the YMCA camp for three weeks, so they were going to drop her off at camp and then spend the next two weeks at a house they were renting near the beach. This would be the first time that Sam could remember going as a family anywhere without her big sister. For two whole weeks, Sam realized, she would be the eldest sibling.

It had only taken a few minutes to get out of Seattle and onto the interstate heading north. Before Sam realized it, Dad had left the road with three or four lanes of traffic in both directions and switched to a small two-lane road that ran along the water. It was sunny when they'd left Seattle, but on this winding road, it seemed to Sam they were traveling through a tunnel of trees. Light flashed through the leaves, as if a bunch of fairies were hiding in the swaying branches above and shining flashlights at them. Sam rode along with her face scrunched up against the glass, wishing she could be a fairy in the trees.

A fairy with a magic wand that could do very interesting things to little brothers.

A few minutes later, the trees began to thin out and the road crested a hill and rolled down to meet the highway. From there, it was mostly through farmland and finally into the small coastal town of Anacortes. Neat little houses lined the streets on the way to the ferry dock, where lines of cars waited to board the massive white and green boat.

"We're here," Dad announced as he pulled the van up to a ticket booth, paid their fare, and got in line behind an SUV.

In no time, a voice came over the loud speakers mounted above the holding lanes. "The ferry to the San Juan Islands will be loading soon. All drivers and passengers, please return to your cars."

It always amazed Sam how big the ferries were. There were several lines of cars waiting ahead of them, and as each took their turn to drive down the dock and up the metal ramp onto the boat, she couldn't keep count. The cars just seemed to keep coming and coming. Finally it was their turn and they were loaded onto the wide metal car deck in one of several neat rows. Their van was in a row nearest the left side of the boat, where large openings in the hull let in light and the salty smell of the sea.

Sam grabbed her jacket and started to pull the sliding door open. She couldn't wait to go up onto the observation deck and watch for whales and dolphins.

"Wait a minute, Sam." Mom's words stopped her in her tracks. "You're not going up there alone."

"I know, Mom. John's coming with me." Sam reached over and tugged on her brother's sleeve. "Come on! Hurry up!"

"That isn't what I meant, Sam. I don't want you and your brother wandering around this boat by yourselves. Your dad and I will stay here with Chestnut. Jenny can go up top with you and John."

As if she had super hearing, Jenny yanked out her ear buds. "Why do I have to watch the rugrats all the time? Sam is going into eighth grade. And John? He's like some nine-year-old genius freak."

"Jennifer Anne Heidleman!" Mom's mouth was drawn into a straight line and her eyebrows were so pinched together Sam was glad her sister was getting the full force of Mom's "mad face" and not her. Even more so because Sam had learned nothing good ever came from a parent using their middle names. Ever.

Even though she doubted her motives, Sam was pleased to hear Jenny stick up for her. John, on the other hand, looked like he didn't know if it was a good thing or a bad thing to be called a nine-year-old genius freak.

"Okay," Dad interrupted in a quiet voice. "Just settle down, everyone." After a calming breath, he went on. "Jenny, I know you want to stay in the car and chill with Chestnut. I get it. But soon you'll be free of your sister and brother for three entire weeks. Give your mom and me some peace and quiet, alone, just the two of us adults, until the ferry lands on Orcas. Okay?"

Jenny took a moment to think about this, then nodded once before squeezing between the center bucket seats.

"Okay. Come on, you two. Maybe we'll see something good in the water today," Jenny said.

The three of them scrambled out of the van.

"And don't call your brother a freak!" Dad called after them.

Jenny led the way up the staircase and ushered them through the heavy metal door to the observation deck of the boat. Sam was glad she'd grabbed her jacket. The sky was blue and nearly cloudless, but it was windy out on the water. She heard the big engines start to rumble as the ferry pulled away from the dock and headed out into Puget Sound. They were finally on their way.

Sam and Jenny leaned against the metal railing with John sandwiched between them. He'd brought his spy periscope along and was turning it from side to side. No one said anything for a long time. They watched grey and white seagulls fly overhead, keeping pace with the boat. A woman farther down the railing reached into a big bag and threw potato chips over the side. The greedy birds snatched them out of the air as they darted past.

"I'm sorry I called you a freak," Jenny said.

John lowered his spy gear.

"That's okay. I hear that stuff at school all the time. My teacher sent a note home to Mom and Dad right before school let out to tell them they want to put me in a special math class next year. The class for the 'smart' kids." John held his fingers up and made parentheses in the air and said the word "smart" like it was a bad word. "She announced it right in front of the whole class, like it was a good thing. I don't want to be different from everybody else." He stopped and slumped over the railing with his head hanging down.

Sam thought about all the times she had been made to feel different from her classmates and put her arm around John's shoulders. Jenny added her arm to Sam's.

"Different isn't bad, John. Different is just… Well, it's just different. Different can even be good," Jenny said.

Sam looked up at her sister. In her way, Jenny was different too. Unlike Sam, she was tall like their mom. She had broad shoulders that were muscular from years of swimming and now rowing. Her eyes, though, were straight from Dad and showed her natural gentleness, even when she was trying to be cool and look tough.

Despite her hair always hanging over one eye, her black leather jacket with all the silver studs and chains, and the heavy black eyeliner that made her look like a zombie, Sam thought her sister was beautiful. Sam had to admit, she really was a good big sister. She'd always been there for her, and even though she sometimes acted like she didn't want to look out for her and John, she always kept them safe. Sam wondered again if she could do the same for John while Jenny was away at camp.

"I wish we could see some whales," John lamented.

"Sorry, kiddo," Jenny said. "The grey whales have already headed north and we won't see them again until they come south in the fall." When John sighed, she added, "But there's a chance we'll see orcas. They hang around here all summer."

"Cool," John said.

Sam thought of these sleek black and white whales, bigger than dolphins, but much smaller than the huge grey whales. Like people, they traveled in families, she'd learned in school. She'd seen them countless times in nature programs on television, but seeing one up close would not only be cool, it would be incredible.

"So the whales are like the island we're going to. Orcas and orcas," John remarked.

"No, they're different," Sam said.

"But they're the same. They sound the same. Are they spelled different?"

"They're spelled the same, but they're different, John." Jenny's voice began to rise.

Sam realized she'd never made the connection before. The words were the same, but they were different. Trust John to notice that.

The ferry dock on Orcas Island grew steadily nearer as the ferry entered a large harbor. Soon another loud voice on the intercom told them to return to their cars.

"I'll explain it to you in the car," Sam told him.

Maybe there was hope for her as a big sister after all, Sam thought.

From Sam's Top Secret Journal...

It's taking FOREVER to get to the beach house. Dad keeps driving down little country roads and getting lost. I never thought Orcas Island was big enough for anybody to get lost on, but Dad's doing it anyway.

I wonder what the house will be like. Mom and Dad rented a condo for us a couple of years ago, but Dad says this house will be much cooler than the condo was. A friend of his stayed there last year and told him about it. I don't know. The condo had a deck with a hot tub. We only got to use it once because John peed in it the first night.

I keep thinking about something Jenny said on the ferry, something important, and I want to write it down before I forget. It's something she said to John. She told him being different wasn't bad, it was just different. Sometimes

being different could even be a good thing, she
said. I'm not sure why I wanted to write
it down. I just did. Maybe it's because it
seems like something I should try to keep
in mind, like something good to know and to
think about the next time somebody tries
to make me feel bad because of my Down
syndrome.

Different isn't bad, it's just different!

I need to stop writing now because it looks
like we're almost there! Yay! I hope there's
a hot tub and John _DOESN'T_ get anywhere
near it!

CHAPTER 2

The Beach House

Dad pulled the van to a stop in a gravel-strewn clearing rimmed with salal and salmonberry bushes. Sam recognized them from the many forest hikes her family had taken over the years. Her dad delighted in teaching them to know and recognize a lot of the native plants that seemed to grow everywhere around them in the Pacific Northwest. Huge evergreens towered overhead and cast everything in a woodsy shade. Through a break in the trees, Sam could just make out a sliver of sky and the white-tipped waves on Puget Sound.

"Where's the beach house?" John asked.

Sam couldn't help thinking the same thing. Where *was* the house? And where was the beach? They were parked at the end of a long and narrow dirt road; even if they'd wanted to keep driving, it was plain from the dense bushes that surrounded them there was nowhere else to drive to. Dad pointed to a sign fashioned from a piece of weathered driftwood propped up next to an opening in the trees. Words were splashed across it in bold, black letters.

"Ravens Roost," Dad said. "This is it. The house is supposed to be right on the other side of these trees."

No one moved. Sam noticed her mother gazing out at the forest with a doubtful expression on her face.

"I know it's not my problem," Jenny said from the back of the van, "but isn't a beach house supposed to be, like, on a beach?"

"It's on a high bluff above the beach," Dad explained. "The people we're renting it from said the view is spectacular and there's a trail that goes right down to the water. It's an easy hike." When no one moved, he threw open the driver's side door. "Come on, you guys! It's going to be great. Everyone, grab your stuff. We'll take a few minutes to get settled in before we drop Jenny off at camp."

Sam took a wistful look at her last journal entry before stuffing the slim book into her backpack and climbing out John's side of the van. Next came Chestnut, tail wagging furiously, a happy dog grin on her face, followed quickly by Jenny. She had a firm grip on Chestnut's leash and looked like she was the one being pulled along instead of the other way around.

Sam knew there was nothing to do but pick up her suitcase and accompany her family down the path through the trees. Chestnut bounded past her with Jenny in tow, followed by John pulling a suitcase on wheels and lugging his camo-colored backpack full of spy gear over one shoulder. Sam took up the rear and tried not to let her heart sink into her shoes with each step along the mossy pathway.

Who builds a house with a driveway that stops in the middle of nowhere?

And was there a house at the end of the trail, Sam couldn't help wondering, not to mention anything remotely resembling a hot tub? For a moment her steps faltered and she froze in panic.

Do they even have TV all the way out here in the boonies?

Just as Sam was beginning to wonder if she would be better off heading to camp with Jenny and living in a rustic cabin with seven other girls for the next two weeks, she reached the end of the short trail and stepped out into the bright sunshine. Ahead of her, framed by a pair of enormous trees with red, peeling bark, was a picture-perfect view of the water and the forested green hills of the other San Juan Islands just a few miles away. To her left, another driftwood sign pointed the way to a path she hoped led down to the beach. To her right stood Ravens Roost.

The house was small—a cottage, really—with sky-blue shingles and white, wooden, shuttered windows on the main floor looking out over the water. On the second floor, the blue and white design was repeated, but with two dormer windows jutting out like big eyes from the steep roof. A path of stepping stones began at a wrought iron gate set beneath an arbor covered with fragrant pink roses.

It's like the house from a fairy tale! She felt like someone had revealed a wonderful secret they'd been keeping just for her.

Sam heard her mother sigh as she opened the gate and stepped into the small yard. A white picket fence separated a neat patch of lawn from the wildness of the surrounding woods. Bright summer flowers filled the borders in a riot of colors. Sam imagined Little Red Riding Hood's grandmother living in the house, or maybe the Three Bears. And here and there she noticed among the flowers small statues of people with red, cone-shaped hats. One was holding an old-fashioned lantern aloft, another sat on a rock and held a miniature fishing pole with a tiny fish dangling at the end of its line, and still another sat reading a book that lay open on its lap.

"Mom, look at the little people!"

Mom laughed and reached down to touch the top of a red hat. "They're garden gnomes, honey. I remember my grandmother loved these. She put them all throughout her garden and I used to imagine I was in a magical kingdom whenever I visited her. I was even convinced there were fairies hiding among the flowers."

Sam remembered how she'd imagined fairies in the trees that very morning during their drive to the ferry dock and tried to conjure up a picture of her mother as a little girl, one who believed in magical kingdoms and mythical creatures. This was a side of her mom she hadn't seen before. It felt good to know she wasn't the only one in the family who enjoyed using her imagination to create fanciful worlds and magical stories. Using her imagination was fun and Sam didn't think being a teenager should mean she couldn't still be creative. It was a big part of who she was.

But Mom and garden gnomes? Who knew?

Sam thought of everything her mom did to keep them safe and happy and wondered if being a mom was so much work you couldn't take the time to believe in magic anymore. If this was the way life worked, Sam wasn't sure she agreed with it.

Mom is more than what she does for the rest of us. So much more. She deserves magic too.

The path meandered to the right and ended at wide, wooden porch. And on that porch stood something Sam had only seen once before in her life, something that split her face in a huge grin as she remembered a visit to her great aunt's house the summer she was going into fifth grade.

A porch swing!

Great Aunt Sarah had called it a "glider." With its green and white striped canopy and wide seat that was perfect for curling up on, it could have been the twin of the one Sam had spent many happy hours daydreaming on during that hot August week in Illinois.

Sam's happy memories were interrupted when John's bag of spy gear hit her in the behind and knocked her sideways.

"Hey!" she said.

"Dibs on an upstairs room!" her brother shouted as he rushed past her toward the door.

"There're two bedrooms upstairs," Dad called after him. "One for each of you. Your mom and I get the big bedroom downstairs. Wait a sec and let me get the door unlocked before you storm the place."

While Mom and Dad went inside the house with John, Sam climbed the steps to linger by the porch swing. Jenny came over and parked herself on one side and patted the other cushion. Chestnut wandered over and plopped down at the top of the steps, her head contentedly draped over her paws.

"This could be kind of cool for you," Jenny said and pulled Sam down beside her. She gave a shove with her foot and the glider swung back and forth in a gentle arc. Sam wondered what she meant; would the glider or the house be cool for her? She'd decided already she liked them both. Then Jenny surprised her by draping an arm over her shoulder and giving her a quick squeeze. "You're going to do great as a big sister while I'm at camp. Just remember that John can be such a complete *pest*. He never lets go of an idea. He'll push like crazy to get his way, even if what he wants to do is a bad idea, maybe even dangerous." She gave the swing another push. "He's smart, but he's still a little kid, Sam." Jenny sighed. "All I'm saying is you have to remember when John pushes, you've got to push back, at least a little bit. Don't let him run all over you."

Sam thought about this as she listened to the metallic twang of the glider's joints and springs carry their weight to and fro. This was the second time that day Jenny had given out advice. In fact, Sam realized, Jenny hadn't directed this many words toward her since the time she'd yelled at her for using her makeup without permission. Sam wanted to savor the moment and think of something nice to say in return, something to let her know she appreciated her big-sisterly wisdom.

Chestnut, unfortunately, had other ideas. Refusing to be ignored, she sauntered over and scrambled onto Jenny's lap, putting an abrupt end to Sam's musing.

"Ew! Dog breath." Jenny pushed herself to her feet and let Chestnut slide back to the ground. "I'd better find some-place for her to do her stinky thing before we get back in the car. And I think you'd better get inside and claim a bed-room before John decides to turn it into his secret spy lair." She gave this last bit of advice air quotes.

Sam stood up too, but before she could think about it too much, she slid her arms around Jenny's waist and hugged her hard. Jenny pulled away.

"Here," she said. Sam watched her untie a friendship bracelet made of embroidery thread from her wrist. "Give me your arm." Sam held her arm out as Jenny tied the brightly colored bracelet on her wrist. "There," Jenny said. "Something to remember me by."

"Oh," Sam said. It was all she knew to say. She looked up at Jenny and she was sure she caught a fleeting glimpse of a smile cross her big sister's face before picking up her bags and following the others into Ravens Roost.

✧ ✧ ✧

It took longer than expected to unpack the car. Just as Jenny predicted, John had deposited his clothes in one of the upstairs bedrooms and his spy gear in the other and was standing in the narrow hallway between the two rooms arguing with Mom that he really, really did need that much space. Every time they went on vacation, John would rush in first to call dibs on the "best" bedroom and then waste everyone's time by not being able to decide which one, *exactly*, was the best. Sam knew how it would end—how it always ended—so she bided her time.

After a minute of total silence that felt like twenty minutes at the dentist, Mom said, "I'll make this easy for you." She marched into the room on the right, picked up John's bag of spy gear, and deposited it on the bed in the room on the opposite side of the hall. "All decided." Then she headed downstairs without a backward glance.

After Mom left, Sam heard John mumble, "This is the cooler room anyway," as he went to unpack his stuff.

Jeez Louise! Sam shook her head at her brother's antics and eagerly began investigating her newly vacated bedroom. It wasn't as big as her room back home, but she liked how cozy it felt at the top of the house, with the walls slanting down from the ceiling on two sides.

It's like a room at the very top of a castle tower!

A wooden desk and chair were bathed in light beneath the lone window. On top of the desk stood a small reading lamp with a shade made of something soft and pink and velvety. A silky fringe on the bottom edge of the lampshade shimmied when Sam touched it. Beside the lamp was a small basket full of shells and colored stones. Sam wondered if they were from the beach down below the house and who might have collected them. She was glad someone had left them there.

Along the opposite wall, a narrow bed was covered in a patchwork quilt, like the ones some of the women at the rec center in their neighborhood sewed for the annual raffle. Sam realized this was the first time she'd seen one up close; her parents didn't have anything like this at home, just regular old blankets. She ran her fingers along the tiny, complicated stitching and marveled at all the work that must have gone into making it. She sat down on the bed and noticed instead of carpeting there were rugs made of braided pieces of fabric covering the plain wooden floor. This house was so different from the house her parents owned in Seattle. She loved her home, but this cottage seemed somehow magical. She liked the feeling she got when the sun came through the bedroom window and the colors on the quilt seemed to almost glow. That feeling was magnified when she went downstairs and checked out the rest of the house. The furniture was worn, but the couches and chairs were the kind that had a lot of stuffing you could sink down into. There was a floor-to-ceiling fireplace made of smooth, grey stones and shelves built right into the walls on either side of it. One shelf was full of familiar board games, like Clue and Sorry, and Sam noticed a few jigsaw puzzles mixed in. The other shelf was full of books all jumbled together. Dad stood nearby, examining their spines. Occasionally he'd pull one out and leaf through the pages.

"Can I go check out the beach?" John yelled from out on the porch. The front door stood open, but Sam was certain they all would have heard him even if it had been closed.

"Yes, you can," Dad said without looking up from the book he was holding.

Mom leaned out of the kitchen doorway. She was putting away the food they'd brought along with them in two big cardboard boxes.

"You have about ten minutes before we leave to drop Jenny off at camp. Sam, you go with your brother." She disappeared back into the kitchen, then popped right back out again. "Better yet, have Jenny go with you."

"But, Mom…" Both Sam and Jenny groaned in unison.

"I'm not a baby. I can watch John on the trail and keep him safe," Sam said.

"We've never been here before. You don't know what the trail's like," Mom said.

"The trail can't be that unsafe or the people who own this place would have been sued like dozens of times by the people who got killed going down to the beach, wouldn't they?" Jenny offered.

Dad looked up from putting groceries in the refrigerator. "I don't know about the likelihood of being sued by dead people, but Jenny does have a point."

Mom glared at Dad for a minute before throwing her hands up in the air. "Okay. But be extra careful. And if the tide's in, don't go down onto the beach!"

"And pie on the way!" Dad called as they left. "Don't forget about pie!"

Sam had to admit pie was sounding pretty good about now, but she was just as eager as John to see what other secrets Ravens Roost held in store.

"Ten minutes. We promise!" she called, as they headed back through the wrought iron gate and over to the sign they'd noticed when they'd first arrived.

"This is the right way," John said, pointing to the letters on the sign. "It says 'TO THE BEACH.'"

The trail disappeared into the trees and it wasn't long before it began to angle sharply down from the top of the bluff. In no time, it led into a staircase made of railroad ties and large rocks that had been built into what was, in Sam's eyes, anything but a gentle slope.

Sam decided now would probably be a good time to practice being the responsible older sister. "Let me go first. In case it's not safe," she announced.

Despite the incline, the trees and undergrowth grew densely and had anchored themselves stubbornly into the soil. Through all the lush greenery, Sam could pick out bits and pieces of water and sky. She could see that some of the trees had even begun to grow out over the water in their search for sunlight and curved out over the water before heading upwards again. Metal pipes were bent and set into the ground at intervals to serve as hand railings, and Sam gave each a good shake to make sure they were sturdy before moving forward.

At last they reached the bottom of the bluff. The trail ended at a wooden dock just big enough to hold a pair of white plastic lawn chairs. A set of concrete steps led down to the water, and all but the top step were dotted with sharp barnacles. When she leaned over the railing and looked down, Sam could see the rocky beach awash under a foot of seawater and navy blue mussels clustered in clumps along the sides of the dark pilings.

On either side of them, the trees leaned out over the beach and concealed the neighboring houses from view. She was free to imagine they were in the middle of the vast ocean, surrounded by uninhabited islands, and the cottage above them was their hideaway on their own secret island.

"Sam! John! We're heading out. Time to come back up." Mom's voice drifted down through the trees from high above them on the bluff.

"I'll race you," John said and bounded back up the stairs. By the time he reached the first switchback in the trail, he'd slowed down and would have lagged behind had Sam not taken his hand and pulled him steadily upwards.

"At least we'll all be in good shape after two weeks of going up and down this hill," Sam said and then chuckled as she suddenly realized she had no idea if Ravens Roost had a TV, not to mention a hot tub. And what surprised her even more was that she realized she didn't care. There was an enchanted cottage, mysterious trails that might lead to adventure, and, best of all, her very own secret island.

From Sam's Top Secret Journal...

I can't wait to tell my best friends, Abby and Sonya, about our cool beach house. Abby's going to . . .

CHAPTER 3

Time for Pie

"Earth to Sam!" Dad cut in. "Put your journal down and concentrate on the scenery. Let's talk about all the fun things we're going to do on vacation instead of just writing about them."

They had settled in to Ravens Roost and were on their way to the farmers market in the tiny town of Eastsound where Dad's favorite strawberry rhubarb pie was waiting for him. It was an annual event: Dad's Pie.

"Well," Sam said, "*some* people are driving *other* people to the farmers market because *some* people want to eat strawberry rhubarb pie while o*ther* people want to write in their journals."

"We can give Dad a break, can't we?" Mom asked. "We're on vacation!"

Sam reached forward from the back seat and touched her dad's shoulder through the driver's seat headrest. "You're the best, Dad," she said softly.

Sam had a lot on her mind. She wasn't really in a bad mood; she was just ready to jump into her own vacation. This was the first time in three years that she had decided not to go to camp, the same camp Jenny was going to work as a lifeguard. At first, when she announced her decision to Mom and Dad, they had tried to talk her out it, but when Sam explained that she wanted to be on her own, they understood. She liked the camp, but she felt she was always following in her sister's footsteps and she wanted her own life.

Sam put her journal away and sighed. Dad didn't get that, for her, writing about what she was doing was important. It was what she did to disappear from the world, a place where she could think and dream. She glanced back at Jenny and made a mental note to ask for a music player of her own for Christmas. Jenny wasn't the only one who wanted to escape!

As they approached Eastsound, Sam could see down to the water and the familiar wooden docks lined with boats. Farther out, the deep blue water was dotted with buoys and brightly colored sails. She noticed how many of the old houses in town looked like Ravens Roost with wooden shutters, white trim, and lots and lots of flowers. Many of them had wooden signs hanging out front on posts.

"What's a 'B and B'?" John asked.

"It means bed and breakfast," Mom explained. "It's like a small hotel in someone's home. They rent rooms out to people and also feed them breakfast. The people have to go out to restaurants for the rest of their meals."

"What we have is better," Dad said. "We get to go away on vacation and we still get to eat your mom's home cooking."

"Hey, don't any of you forget," Mom said with a laugh, "I'm on vacation, too! I think the rest of you could rustle up a few meals while we're here."

John piped up again as he turned around and aimed his spy periscope over the back of his seat at Jenny. "It's a good thing Jenny's going to camp. I don't think I could take another 'cheestastrophy'," he teased.

The image of their smoke-filled kitchen and the mac and cheese that had been burnt to a crisp popped into Sam's brain. It had been Jenny's first attempt at cooking a meal for the three of them one night when Mom and Dad had gone out. It was an epic fail. Since this "cheestastrophy," there had been plenty of opportunities for Jenny to redeem herself with practice and some help from Mom. Now, Jenny regularly made at least one dinner a week. Sam decided that, for now, she was happy just making chocolate chip cookies.

Jenny glowered over the back of John's seat and was about to make a comment, but before she could, Sam jumped in.

"The last time Jenny cooked, I remember it was really, really good. It came out perfect. You remember, don't you, John?" Sam had decided it was time John let the dinner incident go. She leaned over and put her hand on John's arm, squeezing it just long enough for him to lock eyes with her and know she meant business. Mom and Dad had a No Tolerance Policy when it came to using violence to settle arguments, and Sam had no intention of doing anything like that, but she wanted him to know that she was serious.

John looked surprised when the response he'd been expecting came from the wrong sister. His eyes grew wide, and Sam knew she'd gotten her message across.

"Come to think of it," he said, rubbing his arm, "that meat thing she made last week was pretty tasty."

Sam figured that was the best any of them was going to get from John. Jenny seemed satisfied with his compliment and disappeared again into her music. Mom surprised Sam by giving her a wink before turning back around in her seat.

Dad parked a block from the farmers market, and everyone piled out of the van, including Chestnut. Dad tucked his thermos of coffee under his arm and they started on their way. They'd been lucky to find a spot so close as tourists flocked along the sidewalks and hurried to the booths of the market vendors. Sam noticed that almost half the cars they passed had license plates from other states.

Orcas Island really is a special place to visit, Sam thought.

The farmers market was located in a park in the center of town. Two rows of tents contained a wide variety of treats and surprises for the market visitors. It was always a good mix of fresh, locally grown fruits and vegetables, artwork that ranged from oil paintings to welded metal sculptures, and booths of food.

Sam loved to watch the food being prepared right in front of her. It seemed very creative to her and she loved all things creative. There were waffle cones baking at the ice cream vendor, corn dogs being dipped and deep fried, funnel cakes poured into pans in swirly patterns to sizzle in hot oil, and a fun shish kabob stand where you could pick out what you wanted to put on your skewer and they would cook it up on the hot grill. All the different smells from the various food vendors mixed together in one big, delicious cloud of goodness.

Dad's pie tent was right in the middle of the row of food vendors, and he made a beeline straight for it. Wooden shelves lined the back of the tent and each was stacked with fresh pies. A big sign at the front of the tent read, "Strawberry/Rhubarb, Apple, Blackberry." A long line of people stretched away from the booth and threatened to block the walkway down the center of the market.

"Why don't you guys go wander around while Mom and I wait?" he said to them.

Jenny heaved a sigh of relief that she didn't have to hang out with them.

"Can I go talk with the sailboat lady?" she asked.

"Who's the sailboat lady?"

"Dad, you remember," Jenny said. "We talked to her last time we were here. She wrote that book I want to get. The one about how she and her husband sailed all over the world."

"That's right!" Dad nodded. "How 'bout I call you on your cell when we're done here?"

Jenny beamed and trotted off with Chestnut in tow.

"How far do *we* get to wander?" John asked.

"Not so far that you can't hear me when I call for you."

"But we have Sam's cell phone," John whined. "Why can't you just call us when you call Jenny?"

"I could," Dad replied, "but I'd rather you two didn't get so far away you couldn't get back here quickly."

"But Jenny..."

"Jenny is a lot older than you. She's a teenager. And besides, I'm the dad, and the dad gets to make the rules."

John glanced at the ground and Sam decided it probably wouldn't be a good idea to point out she was a teenager too, even though what Dad said hurt her feelings. Maybe she should have gone off to camp. She was tired of being treated like a baby.

Dad pulled Sam in for a hug.

"That was a dumb thing to say. I keep forgetting how old you are, Sam. It's hard for me to get used to how old all of you kids are. You keep growing, and old guys like me can't always take it in. I can still remember when you were a little baby—"

"Dad!" She made a face.

"Okay, here's what we're going to do," Dad said. He let her go and Sam felt the mood lighten. "You two get the same deal as Jenny, but Sam has the added responsibility of keeping you out of trouble." Dad pointed his finger at John and waited until John met his gaze. "You two stay together and I'll call you when we get to the front of the line."

"Thanks!" Sam said and gave Dad a thumbs-up.

No sooner had they been given the go-ahead then John took off running behind the tents and across the park towards the woods. Sam shot off after him, even though running was not her favorite thing. Her awkward gait was just one of the things that came with Down syndrome. In spite of being taller and older than her brother, she was at a disadvantage.

Sam didn't let this get to her. She knew that her training and conditioning from playing basketball on the middle school team and rock climbing every Thursday at Vertical Limit had paid off. Add to this some wild and crazy dancing in her room to her favorite bands, and Sam had lots of endurance and strength. John might win in a sprint, but Sam could beat him in distance.

Down syndrome is a little part of me, she reminded herself. *It isn't the biggest part of me.*

Sam caught up with John at the head of a well-tended trail that led into a forested area. Before she entered the woods, she checked the reception on her cell phone and then slipped it back in her jeans pocket. She felt proud to be the big sister for now.

The path meandered through the tall trees, and like the drive here, the smaller trees formed a tunnel. She could pretend they were walking through a deep, mysterious forest while in reality they were only a little ways from people sitting in the park, eating their favorite food from the farmers market.

The shady trail was damp from recent rain. Puddles filled the low spots in the path and big rocks along the edge looked shiny and slippery. Sam knew better than to try to walk on them, but this didn't stop John. He was wearing his new boots and couldn't resist testing them out on every puddle he encountered.

"Hey, Sam!" he yelled and hopped from rock to rock. "I'm a frog. A big fro…!"

John's foot slid and his arms shot out to catch his balance but he lost it. Down he went, seat first into the mud. He looked up at Sam and she noticed a twinkle flash through his eyes.

"Mom is going to be so mad at you," Sam admonished him. "You've got mud all over your rear end and you're going to get it all over the seat in the van. Give me our hand!" She hauled him to his feet. "Come on, we might as well go back now."

"No, not yet, Sam." John looked over his shoulder to try to get a decent view of his backside. He reached around to dust off the seat of his pants but instead he smeared the mud around. He gave up and looked helplessly at Sam. "If I'm going to get in trouble, how about if I get in trouble later instead of earlier? Besides, the pie line is still probably a mile long and we'll be stuck standing there forever." He held his muddy hands out to her. "Say yes, or you'll be muddy, too!" He made a fake lunge at her.

"Don't you dare," Sam said, pulling back. She thought a moment and then nodded. "Okay, but when Mom sees your pants, you better tell her I had nothing to do with it. You're on your own."

"Deal!" John agreed.

They walked a little ways farther into the woods. John trotted ahead and stopped suddenly.

"Come over and look at this!" he yelled.

A black, muddy blob covered with leaves and pine needles sat happily on the trail in a bright oval of warm sunshine. If it wasn't for its wagging tail, you could hardly guess it was a small dog. It had very long hair that made it look like a dirty mop.

John held his hand out to the little dog.

"Talk about camouflage. I thought it was a pile of leaves!" Sam's brother loved all things camo.

"Does it have a collar?" Sam asked. "I wonder if it's lost. Who would let a little dog like this run around on its own?"

She crouched down, and the little dog licked her hand. Before she and John came up with any answers, a voice called out from behind them, "Molly! Molly, where are you?"

The lump in the trail suddenly jumped up, and four legs and a shaggy head emerged from the black ball of fur.

"Molly!" The voice calling sounded like the voice of a young girl, but no person could be seen.

"Yip! Yip!" Molly barked.

The little dog darted off in the direction of the voice. The last Sam saw of her was her wagging tail and the low bushes shaking as she ran and disappeared beneath the brush.

At that moment, Sam's phone rang. It was Dad.

"Hi, Dad. We're on our way!" she said.

Dad looked happy and satisfied when they arrived. Nothing remained of his strawberry rhubarb pie but a smear of pink on his t-shirt and a few crumbs stuck to his beard. He patted his stomach with both hands.

"I am a happy man," he declared. He put the lid on his thermos of coffee and stood up from a picnic table. "What did you guys do?"

As they walked back to the car, John amused them with the story of the "Camo Dog Named Molly." When he finished, Jenny talked animatedly about the sailboat lady and her plans for a new adventure to Thailand. Mom talked about the mud on the seat of John's pants, although she wasn't mad. Everyone was more easygoing on vacation.

While Mom searched for an old towel in the back of the van for John to sit on, Sam heard a familiar voice nearby.

She stepped over to the sidewalk and saw a black SUV a few parking spots down from them. The doors were open, and a woman with short, curly red hair was standing beside the back door with a girl. The girl looked to be Sam's age and had long black hair that hung straight down her back. Her blue t-shirt was as muddy as John's pants and she wore an unhappy frown on her face.

"Don't make her ride in the carrier, Grace," the girl said. "I promise I'll hold her on my lap all the way home. She won't get the car dirty."

"It's not the car I'm worried about, Tracy." The woman leaned down and put a hand on the girl's shoulder. "The car can be cleaned, Molly can be cleaned, and I bet I can even get the mud out of your favorite t-shirt. I know you want Molly close to you all the time, but she needs to ride in the carrier because it's safer that way."

Tracy grudgingly handed Molly over to Grace so she could put her into the dog carrier on the back seat. As she did so, the dog looked in Sam's direction, recognized her, and yipped in her direction. Tracy turned and for a brief second their eyes locked and the girl looked puzzled. Sam had a crazy urge to raise her hand and wave, but before she could, the girl climbed up into the SUV and they drove away.

"Is that the dog John was talking about?"

Sam almost jumped out of her skin. She hadn't noticed Jenny and Chestnut walk over and join her on the sidewalk. Together they watched the SUV drive away.

"She's a strange one," Jenny said.

"What do you mean?" Sam asked.

"Oh, I don't know. She acted funny with that little dog of hers. I walked by her with Chestnut and she was holding onto that dog like her life depended on it. Then she set her down and it took off and the girl was running all over the market yelling for her." Jenny leaned down and stroked Chestnut's glossy head. "I guess I'd go crazy if I lost Chestnut." The girls climbed into the van after their big dog.

On the drive to drop Jenny off at camp, Dad kept up a barrage of silly riddles. Everyone laughed, even though they were the worst riddles every. Even Jenny giggled from the back seat.

Sam wondered if Jenny would miss them. She watched her big sister scratch Chestnut behind the ears and look seriously out the window of the van. Jenny would have her own summer adventure. For herself, Sam felt light, as though she were full of air and could float away. The sun was shining, it was the first day of vacation, and she was ready to relax and have fun. She was going to have her own adventure, too.

Sam couldn't help thinking about the funny little dog named Molly and the girl named Tracy who she belonged to. There was something about Tracy that puzzled her. She tried to put her finger on it, and the only thing she could come up with was the girl's frown. Her frown looked… Sam searched for the right word.

Permanent.

Well, if a frown could make you strange, like Jenny said, then everybody must be a little strange, Sam thought. *But a permanent frown?*

Sam had no idea what that meant!

From Sam's Top Secret Journal...

I can't believe I thought I wasn't going to like this place! I am writing this in bed while looking at the stars through my bedroom window, and right now, I feel like I am living in a tree house on a secret island. I texted Abby and Sonja and told them all about our cabin. They're stuck in town this summer. They hear the cars on the street through their open windows and I hear the sound of the waves. I am so lucky!

Of course, Mom and Dad and John are here too. Tonight we played board games. So fun! In the afternoon, Dad got his pie at the farmers market. He is so funny about his pie! We each have different things that we love! I had a huge cinnamon roll— yummy! John loves to explore, so we took off while Mom and Dad waited in the mile-long pie line!

John and I followed a trail in the nearby woods. What's the first thing John does? He falls in the mud. LITTLE BROTHERS! The big surprise was discovering a small black dog. A few minutes later, we heard a girl calling for "Molly" and the little dog ran off. It would be terrible to lose Chestnut! When we were getting back in the van with Mom and Dad, I saw a girl about my age with long, dark hair holding the little dog across the street. An older woman who was driving called the girl Tracy.

We dropped Jenny off at camp. I will miss her, but I get my chance at being the oldest! She gave me her friendship bracelet to wear while she is gone. I love her so much, but when Jenny is around, I think Mom and Dad forget that I am a teenager too! When I think about growing up, I think about my Down syndrome more! Sometimes that confuses me, but I know I can do this teenager thing.

I know I can be responsible and I am a good friend. And school next year? Wow, I sure don't have to think about that right now!

For some reason, this all makes me think about the girl, Tracy. I hope she can see the stars from her bedroom window, too. I hope she feels half as happy as I feel. I don't know why I am thinking that, but she seemed so alone. I hope she has sweet dreams tonight! I know I will.

Lights out, more fun tomorrow...

CHAPTER 4

A Haunted House

The next morning, Sam and John and their parents headed down to the beach. Sam's mom had her big bag with a beach towel and a thermos of iced tea, John had his backpack full of spy gear, and Sam had a bag for her beach collecting in one hand and Chestnut on her leash in her other hand. Dad walked carefully at the back of the group with his red kayak balanced carefully over his head.

"You weren't kidding when you said the trail was steep," he said when they reached the bottom.

"Let me help you!" John said and quickly jumped off the trail, landing on the beach below. Dad slid the kayak onto the beach and John guided it down onto the rocky sand. Next, Dad jumped down after the kayak and together they dragged it to the edge of the saltwater.

"Thanks, buddy," he said and gave John's blond hair a rub. John beamed.

Boys and men, Sam thought to herself as she watched Dad and John, *they always have to be strong.*

"We're going to get our exercise going up and down that trail!" Mom exclaimed. She pulled her beach towel out and draped it across a plastic chair on the landing and tossed Dad his lifejacket. Putting on a wide-brimmed straw hat, she pulled out her thick paperback and sat down dramatically. "I am now officially on vacation!"

Mom pulled the brim of her hat down on her forehead and settled in to her book. Sam, John, and Dad knew this was the signal not to bother her. Dad slipped himself into his kayak and pushed off into the gentle waves, and Sam and John took off down the beach with Chestnut in tow.

John paused a little way down the beach and opened up his backpack. "I want to practice my trail signs," he said. He pulled out his survival guide manual and began to gather bits of driftwood and beach rocks, stopping every once in a while to consult the diagrams in the book before arranging the items he had gathered.

From time to time, Sam looked up from her search for beach treasure to check the tide line. In the distance, she could see Dad out on the water. Mom was a long ways down the beach now. Chestnut pulled on her leash and made it hard for Sam to enjoy her beachcombing in peace.

"This will help us find our way back," John yelled over to Sam, who was moving slowly along the water's edge and bent over looking for pieces of beach glass.

Sam walked over towards him, never lifting her eyes from the beach as Chestnut strained against the leash and pulled hard in the opposite direction.

"Don't let her mess this up!" John warned and he jumped in front of his secret sign and waved his arms at Chestnut and Sam.

Sam stopped in her tracks. She knew the rule: Keep the puppy on the leash. It had been Jenny's job and now it was

Sam's job, but she reached down and let the wiggly dog free. Chestnut took off like a shot down the beach.

That dog deserves a vacation too, Sam thought as her eyes followed the bouncing dog. Her decision felt good, but a split second later it felt not-so-good.

"Thanks," John said to his sister. They both stood and looked down the beach after the dog. "She'll be okay."

Sam appreciated his comment.

"What do you think?" he said, nudging her arm.

John pointed down to his creation and Sam took a good look at John's secret trail sign. She knew her brother was the smartest nine-year-old ever, but she couldn't figure out how what she was looking at could be helpful. The rocks and seaweed and sticks looked identical to the bazillion pieces of rocks and seaweed and driftwood that made up the long stretch of beach.

"Doesn't it look a lot like everything else…" she started to ask, but John interrupted her.

"It has to be camouflaged a little. It's a secret sign for just us to recognize. It will help us find our way back."

All we'd have to do is turn around and walk in the opposite direction to find our way back to Mom and Dad, Sam thought.

"Hmm, cool," she said. John beamed and went back to work. Sam knew that sometimes it was better to keep your thoughts to yourself.

Sam and her brother continued their walk down the beach. John kept building his trail markers and Sam had already found six pieces of beach glass, a medium-sized gray rock in the exact shape of a heart, and three small rocks with white rings all the way around them. Mom said rocks with a stripe all the way around were lucky. Just make a wish and throw the rock into the water, she had taught them.

Sam took one out of her bag and weighed it in her hand. What was a good wish? That every day could be as perfect as today? Sam rubbed the rock a couple of times and threw it out into the green waves as far as she could. Chestnut exploded past Sam and bounded out into the water, swimming as fast as she could towards the rippling circles left by the sinking rock.

"Chestnut!" Sam yelled. "It's not a stick!"

The dog swam around in circles, straining to find the non-existent stick, and finally turned in and swam back to shore. She ran out of the water, looking at Sam with questioning eyes.

"It was a rock, silly!" Sam said.

Chestnut stopped and wagged, panting and slobbering as she looked up at Sam. The dog had long trailing green pieces of seaweed hanging on her and she looked ridiculously happy. Then Chestnut shook herself as hard as she could. In an instant, Sam was covered in cold, salty spray, and she stepped back and yelped.

John looked up and laughed. "She sure got you!"

"Oh, you're a good dog, Chestnut! You are just a silly puppy. Good girl!" Sam knew how good positive encouragement felt. She thought for a second how it felt as good to give it as to get it. Chestnut bounded off down the beach again.

Sam noticed that the base of the bluff didn't always match the shape of the water line. Instead, it curved in and out sometimes where the tide had scoured out small caves in the clay. The caves were just big enough for someone to crouch down inside, unseen from above. Sam let her imagination go and for a second she could see the cave as a perfect spot for pirates to hide their chests of stolen gold and jewels.

Out in the water, a line of jagged black rocks poked out of the waves like giant dragon's teeth.

Here is where the mermaids sit to comb the seaweed from their long hair and clean the barnacles from their shiny tails, she thought.

Sam loved the magical feel of the island. She wondered what her friends would say if they could hear her thoughts. She laughed because she suspected both Abby and Sonja would jump right into her game of make believe. That was the cool thing about good friends; they would jump right into anything with you. They would think up goofy pirate names and end up laughing their heads off.

Sam missed her friends and she missed Jenny, too. She fingered Jenny's friendship bracelet and felt better. She was glad to have something to remember her big sister by, even if Jenny was bossy and in her own world most of the time.

The line of jagged rocks caught Sam's eye again, and this time she could hardly see the tops of the dragon's teeth.

"John," she called out and pointed to the rocks. "The rocks are sinking!"

John looked up from where he was up at the bank that tumbled onto the beach with a bunch of blackberry vines and bushes of Scotch Broom.

"They're not sinking, Sam. It's just the tide coming in."

Sam hid her embarrassment with a command.

"Whatever! It's time to head back," she yelled. Sam looked for Chestnut and shouted her name.

"She's over here," John yelled. "Come see what I found."

Sam picked her way over the rocks to her brother, curious about what crazy discovery he had made.

Tucked into the bluff, a set of steps led upwards and disappeared up into the trees. Although the stairs were invisible from the beach, they were sturdy, like the kind of stairs you'd find in the city with concrete and steel handrails, nothing like the simple path and stairs at Sam and John's beach. Tall weeds and bushes formed a gate of green branches across the steps and handrails. Sam couldn't imagine that anyone had gone up or down these steps in a very long time, no matter how perfectly built.

"Where do you think these go?" John asked and hopped onto the bottom step. "Maybe there's an abandoned house at the top. Maybe a *haunted* house!"

The idea of exploring an abandoned house was tempting, but Sam knew it wouldn't be right to trespass. Her parents would have a cow if they found out. Most of all, Sam couldn't help shivering at the thought that there might be a haunted house. She liked the *idea* of ghosts and spooky houses a lot more than actually seeing one up close. She reached down and patted Chestnut's wet head. Suddenly, the bushes whispered and rustled and then the underbrush shook violently and Chestnut let out a low growl.

Startled, Sam jumped down to the beach and John nearly toppled backwards off the step as an inky black shape rocketed across the toes of his sneakers and headed towards Chestnut. It came to a halt and looked up at the big retriever, and a pink tongue emerged from its panting dog grin. The dog's tiny tail wagged and shook its whole body, and then Chestnut's tail wagged, too. Sam scooped up the little black dog and looked at her brother.

"Molly?" they both said at the same time. It was more a question than a statement.

"Man, this little dog gets around," John said, smiling, and scratched the dog behind its wet and dirty ears. As he did, the bushes rustled again the girl with the long black hair at the farmers market emerged from the bushes.

"Molly!" the girl yelled. Her tone was exasperated.

"Hey, we saw you yesterday!" Sam blurted. She immediately felt self-conscious, but she had to admit it was a crazy coincidence.

The girl stood frozen and looked at Sam and John with wide, dark eyes. Sam kept right on going.

"My name is Sam and this is my brother, John. We're staying at Ravens Roost and this is our dog, Chestnut." She blurted this all out in a big heap and felt at a loss what to do next.

She lamely waved down the beach towards their cabin, then realized that she was holding Tracy's little dog. The girl didn't say anything, and Sam quickly reached out to the girl with the black wriggling bundle.

"Here's Molly."

Tracy hugged her dog closely and looked at the brother and sister.

"We were just saying how your dog sure gets around," John said. "We met her yesterday on the beach by the woods at the farmers market. Sort of weird to see her on another beach."

"She really likes to run, but she has never come down here before." The girl glanced over her shoulder back up the hidden steps. "No one comes down here. Not anymore."

The girl hugged the dog closer and looked far out on the water. Sam saw the same worried frown that she had detected yesterday from across the street at the farmers market.

"You live here?" Sam asked. Sam couldn't imagine not coming here every single day if she lived nearby.

"Yes," the girl said quietly and looked back at them. "Hey, didn't I see you at the market yesterday?"

"Yes," Sam said. "Your name is Tracy, isn't it?" Sam explained about finding Molly in the woods and then later seeing Trace and Molly climb into an SUV.

"When we found Molly on the beach, we thought she was a black blob!" John said.

"You're not a black blob, are you?" Tracy nuzzled the dog and stroked her fur. "You're a Russian Tsvetnava Bolonka and very, very special."

"A sweaty *what?*" John asked.

"John!" Sam yelped. It had taken him less than three minutes to embarrass her, although she agreed. She didn't understand a thing Tracy had said. But Tracy smiled a shadow of a smile that didn't reach her eyes.

"Thanks for finding her," she said and looked back up the hidden stairwell.

"I think she's the one who found us," John added.

"Well, thank you anyway. I have to go. My tutor, Mr. Shen, is coming in a few minutes." Tracy started up the stairs but paused and turned back. "Do you guys want to come over to my house? We could hang out after lunch? Around one o'clock?"

Sam hesitated. She didn't know how they would get to Tracy's house later on when the tide was higher. "The tide's coming in," she said. "I don't think we can get back." she scanned the horizon for the line of dragon's teeth and barely saw the tips of the pointed rocks.

"Oh, you can just come down the road from Ravens Roost. It isn't far," Tracy answered. "My house is the only other house on the lane. You can't miss it!" And the girl and the dog disappeared into the underbrush.

Sam wanted to call out that she and John would have to check with their mom, but she just looked up the hillside instead.

The stairs did lead to something, but not something haunted. *Someone lives there*, Sam thought. *A girl with sad eyes and a little dog*. It wasn't a haunted house at all. Maybe it was a castle with a lonely princess at a window that looked out to the sea.

"Come on!" John yelled. "Let's go ask if we can go play with Tracy and her sweaty weird dog!"

Sam hurried after him, but she kept one eye on the rising tide. The dragon's teeth were gone and so were all of John's trail signs. Then she paused.

"Chestnut!" she yelled. Maybe if she got the dog back on the leash, Mom and Dad wouldn't know that the dog had been free as a bird all morning. Chestnut came bounding back to her, and Sam caught her collar and snapped on the leash. Just then, Sam smelled the terrible smell.

"Oh no!" she cried out loud. "What have you rolled in?" There must have been a dead seagull or fish on the beach. Chestnut whined and then wriggled and wagged. "Boy, we're in for it now!" Sam yanked on the leash and the two of them took off down the beach after John.

When Sam and Chestnut got to their stairs, Sam stopped before starting the hike up the steep trail to Ravens Roost. She reached in her bag and pulled out a lucky rock. She could think of two wishes: a wish for a new friend and a wish to not get grounded for a stinky dog. Sam made her choice and threw the rock far out into the waves. Then, she turned and ran up the trail.

From Sam's Top Secret Journal...

I'm writing from the glider on the front porch and everyone else is inside eating lunch. Sometimes you just gotta be alone. Wow, I sound like Jenny! Well, Mom was NOT pleased with the stinky dog and I had to give Chestnut a bath. I used the hose and a bucket of soapy water out in the front yard because Mom was sure Chestnut would spread the dead seagull smell all over the cabin if I put the dog in the bathtub. Dad helped me, but I got all wet and so I am out here drying off and eating and writing.

Well, MY BAD, I made the decision to let Chestnut have some freedom. I guess that's the deal with decisions. They have consequences!

There is so much to tell. This morning on our beach walk, John discovered a set of hidden steps that led up from the beach. At first, we thought it might lead to a haunted house. Instead, John and I met the girl, Tracy, who I saw yesterday! Crazy! Her dog, Molly, ran away AGAIN! Turns out that maybe the stairway leads to a new friend, not a haunted house! Tracy lives down the road and she invited us to come to her house after lunch. Mom almost said no because of the stinky dog thing, but we pleaded with her and Dad was on our side. More later...

CHAPTER 5

The Princess in the Castle

After lunch, Mom and Dad insisted that one of them go with Sam and John to meet Tracy's parents. Secretly, Sam didn't mind. Mom had superpowers when it came to knowing who to trust and who not to trust. It was a though Mom could sense when people's words didn't match what they were really thinking. Sam wished she had a little more of a talent for that. She knew that she could be too trusting and that she didn't always recognize when someone was saying one thing but meaning something else. That usually happened when people were being sarcastic. Even though her teenager self thought it was a little annoying, Sam felt happy that her parents cared about the people she and her brother spent their time with. Sam had a good feeling about Tracy.

A huge hedge of wild rose bushes edged the quiet road to Tracy's house. In the heat of the summer afternoon, the hedge of tiny pink roses gave off a beautiful smell. As they walked along, Sam and her mom stopped every once in a while and took a deep breath.

"That is wonderful," Mom sighed from under her big-brimmed hat. Sam agreed.

"Yuck," said John and kicked some rocks into the road.

When they came to the next driveway and turned in, they stopped immediately. The high hedge had concealed what now lay before them—a rolling lawn and long driveway that led to a huge house. It looked as perfect as a postcard.

"She said we couldn't miss it!" John said.

The house was bigger than any of the houses in their neighborhood in Seattle. Enormous windows that reflected the sun like mirrors and broad decks coming out at all angles were built to enjoy the magnificent views of the water and beach below. The lawn looked like green velvet or as if it had been painted on the ground with a big brush of green paint. Sam had never seen a house with a four-car garage before.

"I feel like a garden gnome!" Mom blurted.

"Without the pointy hats!" John added.

The three of them laughed as they gazed up at the mansion-like house and started up the driveway.

On the porch, John rang the big brass doorbell. The door swung wide and the red-haired woman that Sam had seen with Tracy at the farmers market stood before them.

"Welcome!" The woman took Mom's hand and shook it soundly. "I'm Grace Hardy, Mr. Blakemore's housekeeper." The woman wore a big smile and an apron covered with flour. She looked Mom right in the eye then turned to Sam and John and shook their hands too. "And you must be Sam and John. Come in, come in." She stepped back and waved them into a foyer that was bigger than Sam's living room. "Tracy hasn't stopped talking about you. It'll be wonderful to have some kids playing in this big, empty house."

Grace nodded to Sam and John. It occurred to Sam that Mrs. Hardy was checking them out as much as Mom was checking her out. That was a good thing.

"Such a lovely home," Mom said. Her eyes followed the tall windows above the doorway to the distant ceiling and beautiful hanging light fixture.

"I think it's a little too big, too much to clean!" Mrs. Hardy said bluntly and gave them a wink.

"You can say that again. I wouldn't like to do my chores at this big place!" John burst in. "It would take me an hour to drag the garbage can down to the road."

They all laughed at John's remark. Sam wondered if Tracy's mom would be quiet and serious like Tracy or quick to laugh like Grace Hardy. As if she were reading Sam's mind, Mom spoke up.

"The kids were excited to discover someone close by to play with. I was looking forward to meeting Tracy's parents as well."

Mrs. Hardy's smile faded and she shook her head.

"I am sorry to say that Mrs. Blakemore passed away about a year ago. Mr. Blakemore is away on business overseas." Mrs. Hardy didn't say anything for a moment, and then with great effort she returned to her cheerful self. "It's me and my husband and Tracy holding down the fort. We manage just fine."

"I'm so sorry," Mom murmured.

Sam felt an ache in her stomach and without thinking she took Mom's hand and swung her arm just a little. Sam remembered how painful it had been when Grandma, Mom's mom, had died last year. Mom was very sad and she told Sam that her sadness was big because her love for Grandma was big. Sam thought how bad Tracy must feel.

"Mr. Blakemore has a factory in India that manufactures bicycle parts, so he's away a lot. Most of the time it's just me and Tracy and Mr. Hardy. My husband, Dan, takes care of the grounds and fixes anything that needs fixing." Grace stopped, as if searching for more to say.

The sound of small dog toenails on the hardwood floors filled the new silence and Molly scurried into the room with a loud yip. She wiggled and wagged at John and Sam as though they were old friends. Tracy was close on her heels, sliding to a stop in her stocking feet on the shiny floors. For a second, Sam thought she saw Tracy wiggle and wag a little, too.

"You came!" Tracy said, looking surprised. "Hi, I'm Tracy." She reached out and shook Mom's hand then motioned to Sam and John. "We're going upstairs, follow me." And she slid around on her stocking feet and headed up a large stairway.

"Be home by five o'clock!" Mom called after them. "Will that work for you?" she quickly asked Mrs. Hardy.

"Absolutely!" Mrs. Hardy said. "Come have a quick cup of tea with me while I finish my batch of scones. The kids will be fine."

At the top of the stairs, there was an open landing with big modern landscape paintings on the walls and then a long hallway. Tracy led the way while she babbled to John about her Xbox 360. Sam followed and glanced into the many doors along the hallway. Each room was beautifully decorated and as neat as a pin.

Sam thought about her living room at home with her mom's favorite magazines on the coffee table and the rumpled-up cozy comforter that they shared and snuggled under when they read together. Sam looked for something that would tell her more about Tracy and her family. Back in Seattle, her friends' houses told her a lot about them. Sonya's parents had a whole wall of photos of Sonya in her dance recital costumes, while Abby's walls were covered with Hopi rugs that her parents had brought back from Arizona years before.

At Sam's house, it was easy to find the things her family thought were important: Sam's framed artwork, John's latest science project on display, and Jenny's swimming and rowing trophies. Plus, there were all the knickknacks from their grandparents and souvenirs from her parents' travels before she and John and Jenny were even born. Sam realized that there were clues to the kind of family they were in nearly every room of their home. Maybe that was what made a house a home instead of just a house.

Sam soon saw that it wasn't going to be that easy to find out about Tracy's family. There was nothing on the walls that was personal, only the occasional painting and the gaps between the paintings that revealed mysterious dark rectangles, like phantom picture frames on the wall. Halfway down the hallway, Sam peeked into the doorway of one of the many rooms, where a large bay window looked out over the water. Large overstuffed chairs, a desk, and a beautiful rug filled the room. On the far end, there was a small landing and a narrow staircase that disappeared behind the tall wall. Sam was tempted to walk in and look up the stairs, but she quickly hurried to catch up with Tracy and John.

Tracy and John had their heads together in front of a big-screen TV and they were opening boxes. John looked up.

"She has controllers she's never used," he said in disbelief. "And she has a Wii."

Xbox is such a guy thing, Sam thought.

Mom and Dad didn't let them spend much time playing video games, although they approved of the games that got everyone moving, like bowling or basketball.

"I've got the newest Zelda over here someplace," Tracy said.

"Great, let's do two-player," he said while unpacking another controller. "Take this."

He handed Tracy the brand new controller, but she looked blankly at him.

"I've never played video games with another person."

"Wow," John said staring at her. Sam worried that he was being rude.

"Maybe you could teach me another time." Tracy got up and walked away, picking up Molly on the way and flopping down onto her bed. Molly turned in circles beside her before settling into a ball next to a pile of stuffed animals. "You can play whatever you want to."

"You don't play?" John asked as he scrolled through the menu on a game. Tracy didn't answer and he turned and looked at her.

"I've never had anyone over before," she said softly and scratched Molly's ears.

Sam stood still in the doorway and was relieved that, for once in his life, John didn't say something totally dumb.

"I'll show you any time," he said and turned to play.

Like the rest of the house, Tracy's bedroom was huge. She not only had the wide-screen TV mounted on the wall and a shelf full of games, but she had a computer that she obviously didn't have to share with anyone else in the family.

There isn't anyone to share with, Sam thought.

What really held Sam's gaze was Tracy's bed. At each of its corners stood tall, carved white bedposts that held up a frothy canopy of white lace and ruffles. It was a bed fit for a princess, and sitting there, Tracy looked like a princess.

"Don't just stand there," Tracy said and moved over on the bed as though to invite Sam to take a seat.

Sam sat down beside her and reached over and petted Molly. Molly's tail gave a little wag.

"You really love your dog, don't you?" Sam said in a thinking-out-loud kind of way. Tracy didn't reply, and they both sat quietly for a second. "I'm sorry about your mom," Sam said matter-of-factly. "Mrs. Hardy told us."

"You don't have to call Grace 'Mrs. Hardy.' Nobody but my dad calls her that," Tracy said, ignoring Sam's comment. "They're like my family now. Sometimes I pretend they are my family. I don't know what I would do without them."

"You must have some friends here too?" Sam asked.

"I used to have lots of friends. Before, when we lived in Bellevue, I had a regular life." She paused. "I even belonged to a Girl Scout troop. My mom was the troop leader, and she was great at finding the coolest things for us to do." Tracy scratched Molly's ears again. "Everything is different without her."

Sam hardly knew what to say. Her friends and her family were her whole life. What would she do without any one of them? She thought about all the gossip about boys and the complaining about brothers and sisters and parents that she and her best girl friends did together.

"So why are you here? Why did you leave Bellevue?" Sam asked.

"My dad." Tracy's eyes welled up with tears and she paused. "He didn't want to live in the old house, the house where I grew up. I know he misses my mom, but it is like he's tried to erase everything from that life. So, we moved here. Instead of going to school, my tutor comes over twice a week, and I live here with Grace and Dan." At this, she scooped up Molly. "And my goofy Molly puppy." She hugged the dog and buried her face in its soft fur. "My life has kind of stopped."

Sam thought she heard a touch of anger in Tracy's voice. This was a lot of information to take in. Sadness and anger all at once seemed like a lot to handle. Sam searched for the right thing to say. She'd learned that even when you don't know the right words to use, sometimes the best thing you can say to someone who is sad or hurting is the thing that is in your heart.

"When my grandma died, my mom was so sad." Sam shook her head a little. "I had never seen my mom so sad. And then she said to me that is was okay for her to be sad. And she said something weird, like, her sadness was big because her love for her mom was big."

"It's like math," John said in front of his video game. Without turning or stopping what he was doing, he continued. "Like algebra, each side of the equation equals the other. The amount of happy before is equal to the amount of sad afterward. You wouldn't have the sadness if you didn't have the happiness first."

Tracy looked at the back of John's head and then stared at Sam. Tracy's eyes grew big and she clapped her hand over her mouth. Sam was sure she was going to cry, and she grabbed her hand. Tracy squeezed her hand back and then she burst into laughter.

"Is he always like this?" Tracy asked, trying to control her giggles. "He sounds like a robot!"

"Hey," John said, still not taking his eyes off the screen. "It's simple logic!"

Only John would equate feelings to math and science, but Sam was grateful that her weird little brother could make Tracy laugh.

"Yeah," Sam admitted. "I'm afraid so."

"Hey, John," Tracy said. "Show me how to play this stuff!"

Tracy jumped off her bed and beckoned to Sam. For the next hour, the three of them battled it out at Frisbee and archery. John stayed in a good mood, even though he was the worst shot. Their fun was interrupted by a knock on the door and Grace Hardy came in with a tray of warm scones and butter and jam.

"Enjoy," Grace said with a wink. She set the tray on Tracy's bed and quietly left.

They each helped themselves, and Sam and Tracy left John to a video game and went back to their perch on Tracy's bed. The two of them spread the cloth napkins out on the white bedspread and enjoyed their delicious snack.

"This is like a picnic," Sam said.

"Mmm," Tracy replied, her mouth full. "I haven't been on a picnic in a million years."

Crumbs of scones spewed from her mouth as she spoke, and she and Sam laughed. Molly ate up the crumbs like a little vacuum cleaner. When Tracy's mouth was empty, she looked at Sam.

"Tell me something," Tracy said.

Sam knew what was coming. It was only a matter of time until a new friend would ask, "Why do your eyes look funny?" or, "Why do you talk the way you do?" Down syndrome was an old story for Sam, but a story she knew she'd have to retell for the rest of her life. Sam lay back on the bed and lifted her leg up, touching the edge of the canopy lace with her toes, and she waited. Tracy leaned down on her elbow and faced Sam.

"Do you like treasure hunts?" Tracy asked.

"You mean like looking for Easter eggs or going on scavenger hunts?" Sam asked back. She sat up, surprised at the question.

"Sort of. But looking for big stuff, important stuff. There's something missing and I need to find it. Well, more than one thing. *Things*, actually."

Tracy's eyes were bright. Sam loved a mystery, and what better place to solve one than on a secret island?

"What are we looking for?" Sam asked.

Tracy jumped off her bed, hurried over to her dresser, and pulled open the top drawer. Sam followed her. Tracy reached to the very back of the dresser and pulled something out from beneath a neat stack of folded clothes.

Tracy held a tiny photo out to Sam. The photo had been cut from a strip of photos, like the kind you have taken in a photo booth. Sam and her friend, Abby, had taken a similar photo last fall when they went school shopping together at the mall. Like the best friends that they were, Sam and Abby had laughed and made faces, and the three pictures were hilarious. This photo showed a girl with short dark hair and a young man with glasses. He had his arm around her, and they were leaning into each other and grinning at the camera.

"It's you," Sam said.

"No, that's my mom and my dad," Tracy said and gazed hard at the picture.

"Wow, you look just like her, even though your hair is long and her hair is short. You could be twins."

"This is the only picture I have of my mom because my dad took the rest of them down off the wall. There used to be pictures all over the place, here and at our old house." Tracy smiled for a moment and then her face darkened. "They're all gone now. My dad took everything down because they reminded him of life with my mom."

Sam remembered the dark shadows on the walls in the hallway. It was obvious now that they were from the missing pictures.

"Can you help me?" she asked. "I know they're here somewhere on the property. I just need another pair of eyes."

"Sure we can!" John spoke up. He bounced up from his spot on the floor in front of the TV. It would be impossible to keep a chance for some spy-detective work from him!

"Make that *two* pairs of eyes." Sam smiled and nodded in her brother's direction.

"Thank you so much," Tracy said as she sat up and bounced a little on the bed. "Molly, we have friends to help us!" And Tracy scooped up her dog and gave her a hug.

They three of them made a plan to meet the next morning as Tracy walked them halfway down the long driveway to the road to Ravens Roost. She turned and ran back with her little dog, and Sam looked after her. The big house stood empty and perfect, and Sam thought again about what made a house a home. She fingered Jenny's friendship bracelet on her wrist. Sam knew it had something to do with the things to remember each other by, but it occurred to her that some of those things you couldn't see at all and those things left shadows on your heart.

Sam turned and ran after her brother. The big hedge still breathed the sweet smell of roses, although it was cooler now.

After dinner, Sam thought, *I'm going to ask Mom and Dad and John to play board games with me.*

From Sam's Top Secret Journal...

I'm glad I packed my art stuff. I just made a drawing for Tracy with my colored pencils. It's a picture of her and Molly sitting on her canopy bed. I think I got Tracy's big eyes and long hair just right, even though drawing people is hard! Maybe she will like it enough to put it up on her wall. Those walls have a lot of blank spots.

Mom just called up for me to come down for breakfast. She's making her healthy pancakes with blueberries. John just banged on my door because he wants to get over to Tracy's and help solve her mystery.

There is sand in the bottom of my bed!

Gotta go...

CHAPTER 6

The Attic

The smell of pancakes greeted Sam as she joined her family for breakfast. Dad was devouring the last bits of the tasty treat. He wiped his finger around the edge of the plate to catch the last puddle of syrup and butter and licked his finger with a slurp.

"Dad!" Sam said.

As far as she was concerned, he was showing his worst pie-eating behavior. John followed his dad's example. Mom caught John in the act as she turned around from the stove to serve Sam her pancakes.

"John!" Mom said. "Table manners are not on vacation."

Sam smirked at John as she sat down. She made sure she put her napkin in her lap and politely asked that someone pass the butter. John shot her a look and Sam ignored him.

"What's everyone up to today?" Dad asked as he settled back with his cup of coffee.

"We're going back over to Tracy's," Sam said, looking up at Mom. "I made her a picture." Sam shoved back her chair, ran up the stairs, and came back down with the drawing.

"Wow," Mom said, "nice job!" Mom knew that art was one of Sam's favorite things and she was Sam's biggest fan.

"That does look like Molly," John admitted with his mouth full. "The little black blob."

"Don't talk and eat at the same time, please," Mom said to John. "Give me a hand with the dishes when we're done here. And I would like it if both of you straightened your beds and put your dirty clothes in the duffel bag by the washer. Sam, make sure there aren't any wet clothes on the floor. *Then* you can go to Tracy's."

This was a reminder of yesterday's stinky dog washing chore, and it was John's turn to smirk at Sam.

"I'm off in the kayak again," Dad said. "I was checking the tide chart, and the tide will be in a little earlier every day this week. Make sure you two keep an eye on the tide down by Tracy's stairs. There's no beach at high tide and you could get trapped. The bank is too slippery and steep to climb."

"I'm on it, Dad," John said with his mouth full.

"I'm halfway finished reading my book," Mom said, frowning at John. "Fine with me if you all disappear for a while!"

Sam knew how important downtime was for her. She worked hard to take care of all of them.

Dad cleared his plate and silverware and walked over to the sink. He stopped and kissed Mom on the top of the head as he passed by. "What would we do without you?" Dad asked and smiled. "Plates, everyone. Who's going to wash, who's going to dry?"

Sam and John cleared their plates and went to help.

"Thanks, Mom," they both said.

The three of them got to work at the sink, but they stopped and turned around at a flash of light behind them. Mom stood with her cell phone, snapping photos.

"Gotta have a picture of this!" Mom said. She took another shot while they looked at her and made silly faces. "I'll send these to Jenny! She'll be happy she isn't on the dishwashing crew!"

After their chores, Sam and John hurried up the road to Tracy's house. Sam was glad she brought her hoodie jacket. The sun wasn't out this morning and it was cool. John walked ahead with his backpack of spy gear and his sweatshirt lashed to it. Her brother was always prepared. As they turned up the driveway, clouds passed the sun, and the windows on Tracy's house looked dark and unfriendly.

"Oooh, *haunted!*" he whispered to Sam.

"Stop it!" Sam said.

Tracy and Molly greeted them at the door. Sam and John walked in to the deafening sound of a vacuum cleaner. Grace was hard at work cleaning the living room. She waved to the children when she saw them without stopping her housecleaning.

"Grace is going crazy," Tracy yelled. "My dad is coming home sometime in the next couple of days!"

"That's great!" John yelled back.

Tracy looked blankly at him and gestured up the stairs, and they went up to her room.

Sam and Tracy sat on the big canopy bed and John swung his backpack off, opened it, and pulled out a tablet and pencil.

"What's our plan?" John asked, standing next to the girls.

"You are hilarious!" Tracy laughed. Molly whined and Tracy leaned over, picked the puppy up, and set her on the bed. The dog scurried to the end of the bed and barked at Tracy's big, pink, furry slippers. "Stop it, Molly!" Tracy said.

"No, really," John continued. "We need a plan if we're going to find the missing pictures." He chewed on the end of his pencil and waited. Tracy saw that he was serious.

"I don't think the pictures are in the house," Tracy said.

"Why do you think that? Have you looked in every room?" John asked.

"I've searched every room upstairs and down. And the basement is completely empty except for Dan's tools and the laundry room."

"What about the attic?" Sam asked.

Tracy and John both looked at her.

"How do you know about the attic?" Tracy asked.

"Yesterday," Sam explained. "I didn't mean to go where I wasn't supposed to, but I looked in the big sitting room and I saw another set of stairs." Sam felt a little flustered, but Tracy didn't seem to think it was a big deal.

"I've never been up there," Tracy said. "I mean, nobody said I can't go up there, but the door is locked."

"Let's go!" John said and grabbed his backpack.

Tracy led the way. The room was as lovely as Sam remembered it. A large desk was directly in front of the bay window, and there was a view of the beach and the water. It was a library with cozy places to read and work.

"Way cool!" John whispered. He walked over and looked at the objects on the desk. Everything was arranged perfectly: a knife-like letter opener with a swirly metal handle, a stack of writing paper, and objects that looked like they were from another country. "What are these?" John asked. He pointed to a series of carved animal statues and a wooden box.

"My dad collects things from India," Tracy answered. "He likes carved animals and boxes."

Tracy went over to the steps that disappeared behind the far wall of the room.

"Over here," she said. "Let's double check to see if it's locked." All three of them stepped up the two stairs, looked up, and paused. At the end of a long, narrow staircase was a small door.

"I'll get it," John said. He pushed by them and walked up to the door and tested it. "Locked," he said, looking down at Sam and Tracy's upturned faces. He came back down the stairway, went back into the library, and flopped down into the big chairs. "Let's do this logically. Where would you hide a key?"

"I'd just put it on my key ring," Sam said. She thought about her mom's house and car keys on a big metal loop. "Are you sure we should do this, Tracy?"

Tracy nodded.

"Sure, you could put it on your key ring," John went on. "But let's say that you don't use this key very much, so why haul it around everywhere?" He stopped and gestured to the room. "It's here somewhere."

They sat in silence for a moment. The house was too quiet.

"The vacuuming has stopped," John said.

"Geez," Tracy said. "Grace said she would clean upstairs when she was through with the living room."

Once again, John went into action. He reached in his backpack and got out his trusty periscope.

"Let's see what she's doing," he said, whispering mischievously.

They went to the end of the hallway, and before they got to the upstairs landing, John motioned for everyone to get down on the floor. He lay on his belly and inched out with his periscope to the edge of the landing. John extended the periscope, put it between the handrails, and lowered it down. Tracy and Sam crawled on either side of him.

"Take a look," John said as he handed the periscope to Tracy. For a second, Sam was a tiny bit jealous. That's what she got for teasing him so often about his spy gear! But she'd had plenty of periscope adventures with John over the years.

"I can see into the living room," Tracy whispered. "Oh, I can see Grace. She's dusting." Tracy pulled away from the scope. "That will take her a good hour! We've got time to search for the key."

And with that, the three detectives crawled back to the hallway and returned to the library.

"Let's check the desk," Tracy said.

Sam thought about how Mom and Dad often talked about good boundaries and respect for other people's things. Sam decided to let Tracy open the desk drawers.

The drawers were empty except for a phone book and a few pieces of mail. Sam thought about the desks at her house. The top of Mom's and Dad's desks were overflowing with mail, magazines, folders of Dad's stuff from meetings, laptop computers, and sometimes even Chestnut's leash. Everything was on *top* of the desk instead of *in* the desk.

Tracy picked up a carved box and opened it. The drawer was shallow and held a book of stamps. She shut the lid.

"Wait a sec," John said. "Can I look?"

Tracy handed the wooden box to John. He opened the lid and peeked into the shallow drawer. He softly tapped the sides and bottom, and they heard a hollow sound. Tracy and Sam leaned in as John felt around the sides and bottom of the box. He pushed on one end and a tiny drawer popped open. Inside was a key.

Tracy and Sam both sucked in their breath and Tracy took the key and ran to the stairs.

"I'll take a quick look for Grace," John said, grabbing his periscope and quietly going out to the landing.

"Come on, Sam," Tracy said, and the two girls climbed the stairs. The key slid in easily and the door opened with a small creaking sound. Tracy and Sam looked at each other with wide eyes. "Here we go!" Tracy said.

The room had angled ceilings and two small windows on each side that looked out to the front and the back of the house. Cardboard boxes were lined neatly against a wall, and there were a few pieces of used furniture and a large mirror leaning up against a wall.

"It's stuff from our old house," Tracy said. She walked behind a sofa and dragged her hand along the back of it.

"We'd better hurry," Sam said. "How can I help you?"

"Let's look in these two boxes," Tracy said.

The tops of the boxes were folded closed but not taped shut. Across the sides of both boxes was written the name "Caroline." Tracy unfolded the top of one box. Inside, there was a layer of tissue paper. Tracy pulled it up to reveal a stack of pictures carefully packed and layered with more tissue.

"Looks like we've found them," said Sam.

"Wow," Tracy said, "look in your box!"

Sam opened the second box. It contained clothes, and she slowly pulled out a beautiful shiny dress from the top of the pile.

"Were these your mom's?"

Tracy scooted over to her, took another dress, and held it up to herself.

"They're beautiful," Sam said.

Tracy walked over to the mirror and took a look for herself. She smiled at Sam and slipped the dress she was holding over her head and shoulders and shimmied into it.

"Put yours on, too," she said to Sam.

Sam scrunched up the black dress and pulled it on over her head. The shiny fabric slid easily over her jeans and T-shirt. The girls looked at each other and laughed.

"The dress looks great, but I'm not so sure about the shoes!" Tracy giggled, pointing at Sam's tennis shoes.

"Really?" Sam laughed back and pointed to Tracy's fuzzy slippers.

The girls were still admiring themselves in the mirror when John popped through the attic door. Surprised, Molly let out a short bark.

"Molly, shhh!" John said and picked her up. "Grace is lugging the vacuum up from downstairs." He struggled to talk while Molly wriggled and licked his face. He noticed the dressed-up girls and hissed. "What are you doing? Put those away!"

Sam and Tracy took off the dresses and shoved them back into the boxes. Tracy went to the box of pictures and grabbed two small framed photos.

"Ready," she said and headed to the stairs.

All three of them stood at the top of the stairs while Tracy turned the key in the lock. John handed her the dog and led them down the stairway. At the landing, he motioned to them to stay behind the wall, and he ran to the library door and peeked out.

"She's coming!" he whispered.

Sam could hear Grace Hardy's whistle coming closer down the hallway. Tracy ran across the room to John and stuffed the two photos into a big pocket of his backpack and then hurried to the desk and picked up the carved box. Grace's whistle stopped outside of the library door and the three friends froze.

The door swung open and Grace came in, struggling with her bucket of cleaning supplies and the vacuum cleaner. She stopped abruptly when she saw them.

"Well, heavens," she said, startled by the three kids. "I thought you were playing in Tracy's room!"

Sam stepped forward and pointed to the big desk.

"Tracy was showing us some things that her Dad brought back from his travels in India," Sam said.

Was that a lie? Sam thought. *I am not a person who lies.*

"Ah, yes, Mr. Blakemore likes his collection. He's coming home any day now. Did Tracy tell you?"

John and Sam nodded and smiled. Sam glanced at Tracy and wondered how they would hide the key back in the box.

"Let me help you with the vacuum, Mrs. Hardy," John said, glancing sideways at Sam and Tracy.

John and Grace bent over the cleaning gear and carried it to the middle of the room. Sam stepped in front of Tracy so that Grace couldn't see exactly what she was doing as Tracy pressed the side of the carved box. The secret door slid open and Tracy replaced the key and put the box on the desk.

"A boy with manners!" Grace Hardy exclaimed when she and John had finished.

"Thank you, John." She turned to the girls. "If you don't mind, I need you to play somewhere else while I work on this room."

"No problem, Grace," said Tracy. "Let's go, guys."

The three friends hurried to Tracy's room. Tracy closed the door behind them and leaned against it.

"Wow, that was close!" she said. Her eyes were twinkling and her face lit up with a big smile. "Was that fun or what?"

"Well, we found the pictures!" John said. "Mission accomplished." No sooner had he said this then his eyes wandered to the big screen and the Xbox.

Tracy reached into his backpack and pulled out the framed pictures. "You go for it," she said to John, nodding towards the video games. "Let's look at pictures, Sam."

They flopped onto the bed and each girl took a picture. Sam looked closely at the young girl in her photo. The girl held a basketball and she looked about Sam's age. She had on a team uniform and her dark hair was pulled back in a ponytail. Wisps of sweaty hair stuck to her cheeks and her face shone with pride.

I know that feeling, Sam thought. *I had that feeling when I made my shot in the big game against Forsythe.*

Once again, Sam noticed how much Tracy looked like her mother.

"Your mom played basketball," Sam said to Tracy.

Tracy set down her picture to look at the girl in the basketball uniform.

"Hmm," Tracy said, as if remembering something. "My mom loved sports, but she told me she was really bad at them. She was more of an artist type, but that didn't stop her from playing."

"I play basketball," Sam said. "I don't think I'm that great at it, either."

Smiling, Tracy looked at Sam.

"You have Down syndrome, don't you?" Tracy asked gently. "I mean, I don't want to be rude and bring it up, but one of my friends in Bellevue had a little brother with Down syndrome. I think it's incredible that you do something like basketball. I'm clumsy like my mom, so I've given up on the sports thing."

"I work extra hard at it," Sam said. "My Down syndrome makes some things harder but not impossible." Sam paused. "In a game, it's hard to think fast on my feet, and I run kind of weird. My teammates are totally awesome. They give me a lot of support."

Tracy nodded.

"It's hard to do things completely on your own," Tracy said softly.

Sam looked at her new friend and felt Tracy's loneliness.

"I bet you have awesome friends, Sam," Tracy said to her.

"And they're all a real bother!" John chimed in from his spot in front of the TV.

Tracy laughed at him.

"You sure look like your mom," Sam said. She watched Tracy's smile turn to a worried frown.

"That's why he stays away," Tracy whispered. "That's why the pictures are gone. My dad doesn't want the memories. Maybe he can't stand to look at me."

"Oh no," Sam said quickly when she heard the sadness in Tracy's voice. "Dads aren't like that. Your dad loves you." Sam struggled to say the right thing. She thought of her dad and John carrying the kayak on the beach. "Guys just like to look strong."

"Do you think so?" Tracy asked hopefully.

"Yeah, I do," she answered. "He's worried that if he is sad, it will make you sad, too. He probably thinks he has to be strong."

Molly growled and the girls looked up from the pictures. At the end of Tracy's bed, the top of John's periscope appeared and his voice boomed, "Let's move this mission outside." John's voice sounded like a robot.

Molly went to the end of the bed and barked at the periscope, and the girls' serious mood was broken.

"Good idea," Tracy said, laughing. "I know a hidden trail on the bank above the beach. My mom and I used to walk there. Maybe we could find a place for a hideout!"

"Great!" John said and poked his head up. Molly immediately ran, put her front paws on his shoulders, and began licking his face. "Eeewww," he said.

"Looks like you have a new friend, John," Sam laughed.

"Looks like we all do!" said Tracy.

And with that, the four of them headed out to the woods.

CHAPTER 7

Sam's Secret Island

S am, Tracy, and John hiked across the big lawn of Tracy's house. Once through a large gate, they left the neatly mowed yard and perfect garden and entered a field of wild rose, blackberry, and salal bushes. The sun had cleared a path through the cloudy morning sky, and it shone brightly on the three adventurers. They hiked past the stairs down to the beach but were stopped before they reached the woods by a large patch of stinging nettles. The tall plants stood like menacing soldiers guarding the woods beyond them.

"Wow, no one has been here for a while!" Tracy said.

"Something has been here," Sam said. She bent down and picked up a large feather that had black and white stripes with a touch of gold along one edge. "It's from a Great Horned owl!" Sam exclaimed. "My friend, Andrew, did a report about nocturnal animals and he had a feather like this in his exhibit." Sam passed the feather to the others.

"I think it's a good luck sign," Tracy said. "We'll use it at our hideaway. May I carry it?"

"Sure," Sam said. She gave Tracy the owl feather and Tracy stuck it in her long black ponytail.

John moved ahead of them, swinging a stick and beating the nettles down as he marched forward. "Follow me!" he yelled over his shoulder, and the three hikers continued on their way.

Sam was glad she had worn her long jeans today, plus her socks with her tennis shoes. She was able to walk through the beaten down nettles without getting stung.

"I know that trail starts here somewhere," Tracy said.

"Over here!" John yelled. Sam and Tracy crossed the sunny field. John had beaten the nettles down in a narrow path to the edge of the woods. He was bent over building one of his trail markers when the girls reached him. "Looks like this trail goes into the woods along the high bank."

"Yes," Tracy answered. "This is it. My mom and I used to come here all the time in the summer. I even remember the smell."

Tracy closed her eyes for a moment and took in a deep breath, and Sam did the same. Sam inhaled a combination of all her favorite Orcas Island smells: fir trees, pinecones, yellow grass, and the salty air. The sound of seagulls, waves, and the rustle of the fir trees in the light wind filled the short silence.

"It's the smell of my secret island," Sam said. She immediately felt silly saying her thoughts out loud and she glanced at Tracy. Tracy stood with her eyes closed, as if listening for something in the whisper of the wind. She opened her eyes and smiled at Sam.

"Yes," she said. "You're right, the secret island. Let's go discover your secret island!"

"Forward ho!" John yelled, swinging his stick up onto his shoulder, and they followed the trail into the woods. "Sam's Secret Island straight ahead."

The narrow path traveled along the top of the bank above the beach and was separated from the edge by a hedge of brush. At one point, the bushes thinned out, and they stood at the very edge of the steep bank to the beach below.

"This is a little dangerous," John said.

"Could we slide down to the beach from here?" Tracy asked.

"You'd have to ask the rock climber," John said and pointed to Sam.

"You're a rock climber?" Tracy asked.

"Yeah, my dad got me into it. It was really scary in the beginning, but I love it now. It's made me strong and it helps me focus." Sam stared down at the sandy, clay slope. "You might make it down to the beach if you didn't lose your balance, but there aren't any good hand- or toe-holds. I wouldn't try it."

"I'm going to build a trail marker here to help us remember this spot," John said.

The girls left John to his sign building and continued along the path. The trail dipped deeper into the woods, and the sounds of the beach were replaced by the sounds of the woods. The tall Douglas firs whispered in the light breeze, and birds sang sharply from their tree-top homes. There was the occasional crack and creak of branches bending and rubbing, but there was also a peaceful stillness. The girls walked on in silence for a time, lost in their own thoughts.

"Look at that big stump!" Tracy stopped abruptly and gestured off the trail to a tree stump surrounded with brush. "It looks like it has a face."

"Whoa," Sam laughed.

On top of the stump grew a wild huckleberry bush and thick moss that made the stump look like it was wearing a crazy green wig. Woodpeckers had drilled holes in the sides, and they stared at Tracy and Sam like goofy eyeballs above a round mouth.

John came up behind them. "What's up?" he asked.

"Look!" Sam said and pointed.

"A forest monster," John said.

"Not a monster," Tracy said. "I think she looks friendly!"

"She?" John asked. "It has to be a she?" Sam's little brother was a little bit against all things "girl." Sam could hardly blame him when she thought of all he had to put up with having two sisters.

Tracy gave him a look. "Okay," she said. "He! It's a tree for Pete's sake! Let's go check it out."

The waist-high brush made it hard to move quickly. The girls broke off small branches as they moved forward, clearing a rough path.

The stump was even bigger up close. The top of the big tree had broken off many years ago, and it tipped over at an angle that revealed gnarly roots on one side. There was a clearing around the bottom, and John scurried over the big roots and disappeared.

"Hey," he called. "Over here!"

Sam and Tracy walked around the stump towards John's voice. Under a big root and behind a rock there was an opening that disappeared underneath the stump. John's head popped out from a hole in the tree that was big enough for him to stand up and peek out of.

"Come on in!"

"Can we all fit?" Sam asked.

"I think so," John said.

The girls crouched down and made their way into the snug cave. There was barely room for the three of them to sit in a tight circle. John stretched up and sat up on the edge of the hole in the roof.

"This tree was in a fire," he said. He reached up and chipped off a piece of charcoal from the decaying wood of the ancient tree.

"Maybe it was hit by lightning," Tracy said.

"Maybe so," Sam said. "It's been through a lot in its life."

"And it's still standing!" Tracy said.

John crawled out of the little cave, sat next to the rock, and started writing on it with the piece of charcoal. He finished with a flourish. "What do you think?" he asked. "Sam's Secret Island!"

The girls crawled out of the cave and admired his sign. The writing was uneven and sprawled over the face of the rock, but they didn't mind.

"It's perfect!" Sam said.

"We should fix up the cave!" Tracy said. "I could bring an old blanket."

"We need food and water," John added.

"Some water bottles and some kind of container to hold a snack would be good," Sam said.

"And a flashlight!" John said. "I have a spare one."

"Wouldn't it be cool if we could spend the night here?" Tracy asked. "We'd probably have to put our sleeping bags outside of the cave."

"If we had a tarp and a little bit of rope, we could have extra shelter by the cave entrance," John said. "Then we'd have room."

"Grace's husband, Dan, has lots of tarps he uses for gardening. I could ask him for a small one," Tracy said. "Let's go get some stuff."

"Hmm, I'm not sure Mom would ever agree to let us stay here without checking it out first, and then it wouldn't be a secret anymore!" Sam said.

"You're right about that!" said John.

"Are you guys hungry?" Sam asked. "Must be lunchtime. Do you want to come over for lunch? You could run home and ask Grace and then come over."

"How about we just take the trail?" Tracy said. "It goes all the way to Ravens Roost. Before your cabin was a rental, it belonged to my mom's friend, Mrs. Cameron. We used to visit her and we took the trail to her house. Do you think your mom and dad would mind if I just showed up?"

"Let's find out," Sam said. John and Tracy started to climb out of the cave, but Sam stopped. "Wait!" They came back and sat next to her. "Are we going to tell anyone about Sam's Secret Island?"

They sat together for a moment in the cave. It was cool on the dry dirt, and the old stump smelled like sawdust and pinecones. Sam wondered if they were the only people who had ever sat there.

Tracy interrupted the quiet. "Let's keep it to ourselves. Dan and Grace will never notice a tarp missing or a blanket."

"I can grab a water bottle from the recycle bin at the cabin," John said. "No one will miss that!"

"So, it's a secret?" Sam asked again.

Tracy and John nodded and smiled.

"Everyone stick out your hand!" John commanded. He took the piece of charcoal and made a small "X" on top of each girl's hand and then on his own. "Our secret pact."

They climbed out from under the stump and started down the trail, but Sam paused and looked back.

Sam's Secret Island, she thought. *It's funny how wishes can come true.*

☆ ☆ ☆

"Hi, Mom," Sam called out as she pushed through the door of Ravens Roost. "We're back!"

"I'm in the kitchen!" Mom answered. The kids went to the kitchen where Mom was making sandwiches at the counter. "How is it you two can't keep track of time but you always show up for food?" she said over her shoulder.

"We're basically animals," John said matter-of-factly.

"Three animals, actually," Sam said.

Mom turned around and smiled when she saw Tracy.

"Good to see you again. Can you have lunch with us? The kids' dad is just coming up from kayaking."

"Yes, thanks. May I call Grace?" Tracy asked.

"Sure," Mom said.

Tracy checked in with Grace and they all sat down at the table. Mom asked them about their morning. The kids told them about hanging out at Tracy's and how they had discovered the trail along the bank above the beach. She was interested to know that it went all the way to Tracy's house. They said nothing about the attic adventure or the secret hideaway. Sam felt a little strange not telling her mom all the details of the morning, but she felt excited about having her own adventure and knew Tracy and John felt the same way too.

Just before they finished, Dad came in.

"We have company," Mom said.

"So I see." Dad bent down and kissed Mom on the head. "Is this the famous Tracy?"

Tracy blushed a little and nodded her head.

"It's nice to meet you," she said. Tracy's eyes followed him.

Sam's dad sat down and grabbed the last sandwich. He looked happy and sunburned. Sam wondered what Tracy thought of their little family. Suddenly Sam missed Jenny. Tracy would love Jenny, with her black eyeliner and her cool style. But when Sam glanced at Tracy, she saw a worried look on her face.

Maybe all this family is too much for her, Sam thought.

"Tracy's dad is coming home soon," Sam blurted. "How long has he been away, Tracy?"

"It's been awhile this time," Tracy said. "Almost a month, I think. He always says that it will be shorter next time, but the trips just get longer." She wadded her paper napkin up and pushed back her plate.

"Dads work hard for their families," Mom said. "I'm sure that he hates being away as much as you hate having him away."

"I've gotten used to it," Tracy said. The tone in Tracy's voice sounded like Jenny. Jenny could say one thing and Sam could be pretty sure that underneath she meant just the opposite.

"It probably takes a lot of time and energy to keep a business going," Dad chimed in. Sam looked at her dad. She thought he sensed Tracy's mood change, and he quickly changed the subject. "I think the tide will be perfect for swimming later this afternoon."

"Dad!" Sam and John groaned at the same time.

"What?" he asked.

"You're the only person in the whole world that likes swimming in this water," Sam said.

"You and a couple of polar bears!" John said.

"My mom loved swimming in salt water. I haven't done that for a long time," Tracy said. She grabbed her wadded-up paper napkin and nervously played with it in her lap.

"Well, I think four o'clock will be the perfect swim time. Almost high tide and the water will have had all day to warm up! Anybody with me?"

Sam looked at Tracy, who was smiling at the idea. She kicked John under the table and gave him a quick nod.

"Why not, Dad?" John said. "The first swim of the summer. Guess it's gotta happen sooner or later."

Sam's family and Tracy laughed together.

Going swimming to help out a friend, Sam thought. *That's not so hard.*

And Dad would be happy, too!

From Sam's Top Secret Journal...

I'm going to sleep like a rock tonight. That's what swimming in the saltwater does to me, especially in this freezing water. I have to admit it was fun! Tracy loved it, and I can tell she likes hanging out with my family. I can't imagine what it would be like to be alone as much as she's been.

Before we met Dad for some swimming, we worked on our hideout. Tracy brought the pictures of her mom and built a special spot for them in the cave. We have some water bottles and we stored some snacks in a shoebox. First thing in the morning, we will meet there and do some more work! It's looking pretty cool!

Jenny has a day off this week and she is coming home for dinner. I don't know if I want to tell her about Sam's Secret Island! I miss her and I don't miss her at the same time. Is that even possible? More later...

High Tide Trouble

"I hope the weather stays nice for Jenny's day off tomorrow," Mom said. "Maybe we could have a picnic on the beach?"

"Sounds fun," Dad said. He flipped a page in his kayaking magazine and took a sip of his coffee.

John was munching on his cereal and staring at the back of the cereal box.

"Supposed to rain tomorrow," he said.

Sam looked over at her mom.

"Do you think Tracy could come over for dinner and meet Jenny?" she asked.

"Let's keep it family. Tracy was just here for lunch and a swim."

"Yeah, I guess so," Sam said. She didn't really agree with her mom. Sam felt lucky that she had someone to hang out with during her vacation week at Ravens Roost, and she wanted to spend as much time with her new friend as possible. It would have been a long week away from her friends in Seattle with just John to hang out with.

"You ready to go?" John asked Sam. He pushed back his chair and took his dishes to the sink.

Before Sam could answer, Mom chimed in, "Take Chestnut with you today."

"*Mom*," John moaned.

"What's so important that the dog can't come along? Where you guys going?" Mom asked.

Sam and John looked at each other.

"We're going to meet Tracy," Sam blurted. "The beach, maybe!"

"Great, Chestnut loves the beach!" Mom said. "Don't forget her leash."

Sam and John gave each other a look as they gathered up their stuff and the dog. What could they say? Sorry, we're going to our secret hiding place and we don't want you or the dog to know anything about it?

"Don't know if we'll be back for lunch," John said. "We might eat at Tracy's."

Mom looked up from her poached egg breakfast. "Just check in later."

Sam tried to think if she had ever seen her mom sitting down at breakfast when both she and John were done eating. At home, when they weren't on vacation, it was a big rush after breakfast to get themselves into the car while they figured out lunch money and afterschool pick-up times. Even Chestnut was in on the chaos, because Mom always took her for a short run after she dropped Sam and John off at their different schools.

Moms have the hardest jobs in the whole world, Sam thought.

Sam, John, and Chestnut hurried on their way. At the end of the driveway, they glanced back at Ravens Roost to see that Mom and Dad weren't on the front porch, and then they ducked into the woods. Sam let Chestnut off of her leash and Chestnut took off down the trail.

They heard dogs barking up ahead and a moment later they came upon Tracy and Molly.

"That's funny," Sam said. "Did you get the dog order, too?"

"Yes. Grace said Molly whined all afternoon yesterday when I was gone. She said she wasn't putting up with that again," Tracy answered. "Can't blame her." She set Molly down, and she and Chestnut put their noses to the ground and ran into the brush.

"Grace or Molly?" John asked.

Sam and Tracy rolled their eyes at each other. The dogs began barking again, and the kids set off after the noise. Molly and Chestnut had followed their noses to the turn-off to Sam's Secret Island. They were stopped on the narrow trail and barking furiously.

The kids came up behind them. Clinging to the top of the tree stump, a squirrel stared straight at the dogs. It was stretched out with each foot clinging tensely to the stump. Its furry tail stood straight up and its beady eyes focused on the dogs.

"Chee, chee, chee, chee," the squirrel chattered. It was a loud and rapid cry, and with every chirp, the squirrel's whole body jerked.

Chestnut and Molly both whined and took one step closer.

"Chee, chee, chee, chee," the squirrel continued.

"Wow," John said. "We have a guard squirrel. What do you think of that?"

"Are we going to be able to get in the hideout?" Tracy asked. "He looks pretty serious!"

"Let's see," said Sam. She walked ahead of the dogs, and they followed. The squirrel's chattering stopped and suddenly it jumped straight up in the air, shook its tail, and disappeared down the side of the stump into the underbrush. The dogs ran after it, but the brave little squirrel was too quick for them. Sam climbed over the roots and entered the cave.

"Oh no!"

"What?" Tracy asked. She and John scrambled in after her.

Sam didn't have to say anything. The cardboard box that held the snacks was shredded, and bits and pieces of cardboard littered the floor of the cave like new-fallen snow. Sam picked up what was left of a granola wrapper and held it up for the others to see.

"Looks like we spoiled that squirrel's party!" she said.

"No wonder he was so mad. I guess he was super hungry!" Tracy said, laughing.

"What about me when I get super hungry?" John said. "Well, let's clean up this mess. We need a different kind of container. Plastic maybe, or metal. Metal is what they used to use to bury a cache of food out in the wilderness. You can see how cardboard doesn't work so well. Imagine bear or big wildlife!"

"Don't tell me there are bears out here!" Sam said.

"No way, a deer maybe," Tracy said.

The kids gathered up the squirrel garbage and John put it in a pocket of his backpack. When he was done, Tracy reached into her backpack pulled out a small blue tarp and some rope.

"See if you can't put up a covered outdoor area," she said.

John jumped at the opportunity to work on a project and took the tarp and rope and disappeared out of the cave.

Tracy sat back down and watched Sam take a folded piece of paper out of her back pocket. It was one of her drawings, and Sam looked around for a place to put it.

There was a little broken branch that stuck out and Sam stabbed it through the upper edge picture and it hung, sort of, on the wall.

"What did you draw?" Tracy asked.

"Look," Sam said. She straightened the piece of paper on the branch and sat back.

"It's us swimming yesterday!" Tracy said. "And there's your dad playing lifeguard in his red kayak. Not bad."

"Thanks," Sam said.

For the most part, Sam didn't like to share her art, even though drawing was her favorite thing to do. When she was drawing, she never thought about what other people would think about her work; she just did it. She could be lost in drawing for a long time. There were so many decisions to make when she was working on a picture: colors, shapes, what to leave in a picture, and what to leave out. When she finished, she felt like she was waking up from a dream world.

If others wanted to see her work or comment on it, she felt self-conscious and nervous. Mom and Dad told her over and over again that it didn't matter what anyone else thought of her artwork. In her head, Sam knew this was true, but in her insides, it didn't feel true. She felt brave putting her picture up in the cave.

"You really love your family!" Tracy said. "I know why. They're so much fun."

"Most of the time, I guess," Sam said.

"I'd never draw a picture of my dad."

"Really?" Sam asked. Suddenly she wondered if she was being too babyish drawing a picture of her family.

"He's gone so much now," Tracy said. "When he comes back today, or whenever he does show up, we have to get to know each other all over again."

Sam thought about how her dad showed up at home every night. Sometimes his life as a surgeon was really crazy and he would get there very late, but he always came home. Sam had memorized the sound of his car in the driveway, the way he slammed the back door and called Mom's name, and even how his footsteps sounded on the wooden floors of their house. You could always tell when Dad came in; the household got happy.

"Maybe it won't always be this way," Sam said. "Last winter vacation, the holidays were hard at our house because Uncle Alex was in Afghanistan. This holiday, he'll be back and we can be together again. Stuff changes."

"Maybe," Tracy said. The two friends sat in silence for a minute. "I'm afraid he'll send me away."

"Away?" Sam said. She sat forward and looked closely at Tracy. "What do you mean 'away'?"

"He freaks out about my grades in school. Particularly math; I'm terrible at it."

"I know that one!" Sam said.

"No, really, I'm major bad at math. I'm a whole grade level behind, even though I have my tutor." Tracy stopped talking, picked up a little rock, and threw it against the ground, then picked it up and threw it again. "Dad said this summer, if I don't get caught up, he will send me to private school in the fall. Private school. I mean, where would that even be? I can't go away again. All we do is go away. I'm too far away from everything as it is!" Tracy clutched the rock and burst into tears.

Sam listened to her friend sobbing and didn't say a word. Tracy wiped her nose on her hand and looked at Sam.

"You're a good friend, Sam," Tracy said. "I don't know how I would have made it through this summer without you and John showing up."

Sam still didn't know what to say. Instead, she reached down to Jenny's friendship bracelet and untied the knot in the turquoise and orange string. She took it off her wrist and held it out to Tracy.

"Here," Sam said.

"You can't give me that. It was your sister's," Tracy said, but she held out her wrist.

Sam was happy to give her the bracelet, but she had a moment of panic when she thought about tying a new knot. Tying anything was a big challenge for her, and she had worked so hard since she was young to get it right. Tracy seemed to notice her worry.

"Can I help?" she asked.

Sam paused and then confessed. "Tying knots is crazy hard for me," she murmured.

Tracy tied the bracelet onto her wrist, but she had to use her teeth to hold one end of the embroidery thread. "You're right, Sam, this isn't easy!" The two friends laughed as Tracy admired the gift.

"Something to remember me by," Sam said.

"You're the best," Tracy said as she fingered the bracelet and smiled.

"Hey, come on out here!" John yelled from outside the cave.

The girls climbed out. John had strung the tarp up between the stump and a small tree. It created a covered area that had more space than was in the cave.

"We need a good board to make a bench to sit on," John said. "We could prop up one end on that rock and the other on this little stump."

"Yeah," Sam said. "It's pretty dusty sitting in the cave." She brushed off the seat of her pants. "Maybe the cave is our special storage area or meeting place and we can live outside here. We can go in the cave when we need to hide."

"Good idea," John said. "I was thinking if we had some kind of plastic jar we could bury it and keep that crazy squirrel out of our food supplies. Who knows what other animals we might attract next time? Raccoons, maybe, or an otter."

"I bet we'd find something down on the beach," Sam said. "There's always stuff like that in the driftwood. We don't have anything like that at the cabin, and we don't want Grace and Dan to get suspicious if their stuff keeps disappearing."

"Well, what are we waiting for?" John said. "To the beach!"

"Let's take my stairs," Tracy shouted. "I think the dogs went that way."

"Chestnut!" Sam yelled. The two dogs came bursting down the trail. Chestnut's tongue hung out, and Molly, as usual, was covered with sticks and leaves. "Well, you two are having fun!"

The kids and dogs moved briskly along the trail towards Tracy's house. They paused where John had placed the trail sign to mark the edge of the bank. Looking down, they could see the beach. Clouds were on the horizon and the wind had picked up, making the water look gray and rough.

"Maybe I should check my tide chart," John said. "I think the tide is coming in."

"No!" Tracy said. "Let's just hurry. I bet we can find a board pretty quick in all that driftwood."

They agreed and headed to the steps. The dogs went down first and ran down the beach towards Ravens Roost. Sam saw them stop and sniff around the place where she'd seen the dragon's teeth in the water. The tips of the pointy rocks were barely visible, and gray waves crashed and splashed against the tops of the rocks. The dogs were a long ways down and had to jump up on the driftwood now, as there was no more sand to run on, just the incoming tide.

"Over here," John yelled.

Sam jumped up onto the driftwood. There were tons of logs, all turned silver now from years in the sun and rain on Orcas. It was tricky walking along the narrow logs and jumping to the next foothold. It reminded her of the time she had tried to walk on a balance beam. Sam was grateful for all her rock climbing, good balance, and strong legs.

"Look," John said. He pointed up the sandy bank. "I think that's where the trail is exposed. Sam's Secret Island is right up there. No one can see it from the beach!"

Sam looked up. The bank wasn't very high, but it was steep and it would be nearly impossible to climb up.

"I guess we'll be safe from pirate invaders," Sam yelled. She had to yell, as the wind and waves were pounding very near them now.

She looked up to see Tracy near the bank pulling on a big board. Tracy gestured to Sam and John. They climbed over the driftwood to reach her. She was wrestling with a plank about twelve inches across and four feet long.

"This will be perfect," John said. "Here, let me take this end. Sam, make sure the dogs are following us. Let's go."

Sam yelled for the dogs, but she didn't see them. She walked down to the edge of the water and realized there was no beach left. In the distance, Sam saw the bobbing heads of Chestnut and Molly wading or swimming in the water towards Ravens Roost.

"Chestnut, Molly!" she yelled. She knew the dogs couldn't hear her over the wind and the waves.

We're in for it now, Sam thought. *Those dogs will go straight up the trail to the cabin.*

She turned to walk back to the steps and stopped.

The beach was gone.

Sam looked up to where John and Tracy were wrestling with the plank, and she realized they were concentrating on their feet and hadn't realized that they had no place to go. Sam hurried over to them.

"You guys, look!" Sam pointed.

Ahead of them, the driftwood stopped and there was nothing but water. The bank came all the way down to the beach in a sort of point, and the piles of driftwood ended. The water crashed against the bank with rough waves.

"The tide's not that high," John said. He squinted at the water. "We'll have to wade. Come on, help us with this."

The three of them lugged the heavy plank to the end of the driftwood and then dropped it into the water. Beyond the bank, they could see Tracy's stairs. Waves were crashing against the bottom step.

"We can float the board in the water," John said. "It'll be a lot less work. Come on."

He stepped into the water alongside the big piece of wood and sank up to his waist.

"Whoa!" he yelped.

"Be careful!" Tracy yelled.

"Brrr, it's colder than yesterday," John said. "Hurry up, this is our only chance."

The girls followed after him, and they pushed the floating board in front of them. As they walked toward the point, the sand beneath their feet became rocky and slippery. They couldn't even see their feet. They slowed down as they felt their way over the rocks. There was a big splash behind Sam, and she turned around to see John fall under the water.

John bobbed up and smiled.

"Oops!" he laughed. He stood up and fell over again. Sam could see that his clothes were heavy with the saltwater. The wind was strong now and the waves seemed to push harder against them as they continued walking.

"Take off your jacket, John," Sam yelled. "Put it on the board. It's weighing you down."

John struggled out of his jacket and then reached down and took off his hiking boots and held them above his head. Tracy and Sam watched him. They were all in above their waists now and swimming seemed like the only choice.

"If we hold onto the board and we all kick, we can make it," Sam said. She did not feel afraid, but she was very cold. When they swam in the cold water yesterday with Dad, the sun was out and it felt warm. Today was a different story. "We need to go out a little and then around the point," Sam said. "Otherwise the waves are going to crash us into the rocks."

The three kids piled their shoes on the board, grabbed an edge, and started kicking. Sam felt her feet leave the bottom and she kicked hard. Immediately, she felt warmer as she worked hard to swim to shore. She didn't want to know how deep the water was now. She only knew that it was getting deeper by the second.

"Oh no," Tracy cried. "My shoe!" One of her shoes fell off the board, floated for a moment, and then sank.

"Keep kicking," John yelled.

They kept going, but they were moving slowly. Suddenly, they heard a familiar voice.

"Sam!"

The kids looked over their shoulders to see Dad in his kayak paddling hard to catch up with them. Sam stopped kicking and waved at him. As she did, her glasses slipped off of her nose. She made a grab for them, briefly going underwater and coming up coughing. Dad pulled up next to them.

"The three of you! You hold on and don't let go. Whatever you do, do not let go of the board." Dad reached behind him and grabbed a coiled rope and yelled to John. "Take this, buddy, and don't let go. There's a loop in the end of it that you can hold onto. I'll drag you all to shore."

Dad's voice was calm and direct, but Sam recognized it. It was his emergency voice, and she knew they had to do exactly as he said. Dad paddled hard against the wind and waves, but after a few moments, the heavy load began to move with the tide and the red kayak pulled them slowly towards Tracy's beach stairs.

"Who's that?" John said to Tracy. He kept kicking but jerked his head towards the stairs.

Tracy and Sam saw a man near the beach stairs. He was yelling and waving his arms as he waded in the water. Even from a distance, they could see that he was very upset.

"Oh no!" Tracy moaned.

"Who is it?" Sam gasped.

"It's my dad," Tracy said.

Sam wasn't sure how Tracy could look any more miserable than she did soaking wet and freezing to death.

But she did.

CHAPTER 9

The Rainy Day

Sam stared out the back window of the van as they drove to pick up Jenny. Gray rain fell straight down, and summer seemed to have disappeared. The wet road hissed and the windshield wipers beat a sleepy rhythm.

Sam and John were grounded, and no one in the van was talking.

Until yesterday, this week on Orcas Island had been the best vacation of Sam's life. She knew it was a combination of things: the cozy cabin at Ravens Roost, her chance at being the big sister in the family, and her new friend, Tracy.

This short week made her feel that she had changed, and she loved the feeling. But today, sitting in the back seat of the van, Sam felt like a prisoner. Each person in her family sat in their usual place, and soon Jenny would be sitting in hers. The van felt like her old life in town: the crazy busy schedule and the constant "doing" of everyday life. It was as though she had outgrown it all like an old pair of jeans.

And yesterday! There wasn't anything worse than angry parents. When Sam saw the dogs disappear down the beach, she knew they were going to get in trouble for their beach adventure. Sure enough, when Chestnut and Molly showed up at Ravens Roost, soaking wet and without her and John, Mom and Dad were worried. Worst of all, it was a terrible way to meet Tracy's dad. Mr. Blakemore had yelled at Sam and John for being irresponsible, grabbed Tracy's arm, and dragged her up the stairs to the house.

Dad stepped in and calmed things down a bit. He called Mom at Ravens Roost, and she drove up to Tracy's and picked them up and stayed and talked to Tracy's dad. Later, Sam and John tried to explain that they were swimming instead of wading because they thought it would be easier to get to Tracy's beach stairs. Sam made it clear that they were never out in the water over their heads.

In spite of Sam's explanation, Mom was angry. John kept saying it was no big deal, and that made Mom even madder. When all was said and done, being grounded for one day seemed fair enough considering the worry they had caused their parents.

"Wish we had a better day for Jenny's visit," Mom said. Her voice broke the silence in the van, but no one answered. John, who was staring at his survival guide, snuck a glance at Sam and rolled his eyes.

He feels trapped, too, Sam thought.

Dad turned and drove in on the long dirt road to Jenny's camp. Out the window, Sam could see a group of kids in rain gear sitting on logs and another line of younger kids following a leader along a trail in the woods.

We made our own camp, Sam thought.

They pulled into a parking lot in front of the lodge, and Sam could see down to the beach and the swimming area. That was where Jenny worked as a lifeguard. Her sister was an awesome swimmer and got along well with other kids. Plus, she was bossy enough to make kids follow the rules and be safe.

Suddenly, Sam felt excited to see her sister.

She didn't have to wait long. Jenny ran up to the car, her backpack over her shoulder and a smile on her face. Her face was tan from lifeguarding, and her blue eyes sparkled without her usual black eyeliner. Her hair was wet and pulled back in a ponytail.

"Hey, girl!" Dad jumped out of the car and smiled a big grin. Mom opened her door and gave Jenny a quick hug and then opened the back door of the van.

"Hi!" Jenny said. She climbed in past John and Sam and threw her arms around Chestnut. "How's my big dog?" She scratched Chestnut's ears with both hands, and the dog's tongue hung out and she slobbered.

"She's been pretty happy on the beach and in the woods with Sam and John," Mom said, turning around and smiling at her oldest child. "How's it been at camp?"

Dad backed up the van as they all waited for Jenny's answer. She looked out the window, still scratching Chestnut's ears.

"It's been really good. Hasn't the weather been awesome? I mean, until today," Jenny answered. "I share the bunkhouse with two other girls who lifeguard. Mom, do you remember Linda Adamson from rowing? Well, one of my roommates is her neighbor. Small world, huh? And there are some cool guys, too. One guy, we call him Gus, his dad is a doctor, a surgeon down in Tacoma. He shares his playlist with all of us. Really cool music." Jenny took a deep breath and paused.

John turned around and looked at his sister. "That's more words than you said to us all last year. Are you really Jenny Heidleman?"

Jenny laughed and blushed. Sam, Mom, and Dad waited. "Well, you asked," she said. Jenny kept petting Chestnut and sat back and looked out of the window. "I'm looking forward to a real dinner. Camp food is a little weird."

John was right. There was something different in Jenny's voice. She was more positive and talkative.

Jenny's changed, too, Sam thought.

"We're having your favorite, mac and cheese," Mom said. "Seems like a day for it. We're going to stop at the farmer's market and get a pie for dessert."

"PIE!" Dad yelled.

Some things don't change! Sam thought.

They drove into town and parked at the market.

"Who's coming to get the pie?" Dad asked.

"I'll go with you," John said. Sam could tell he was already overwhelmed with sisters.

"I need to grab a few things from the grocery store," Mom said.

"My hair's wet," Jenny said. "I'll stay."

"Sam?" Mom looked into the back.

"I'm staying."

With that, the doors slammed and the shoppers went off in different directions. Sam thought for sure that Jenny would put on her headphones and disappear into her music, but she didn't.

"And you, Sam?" Jenny asked. "What's going on with you?"

Sam wasn't interested in answering the question. She turned and faced the back seat and she asked one instead. "You look different. No eyeliner, no black jacket?" Sam looked closely at Jenny. She saw a wistful look on her sister's face with a small smile. It sure wasn't a Jenny look! "Do you have a boyfriend?" Sam blurted the question before she could even think about it.

Jenny laughed and Chestnut wagged her tail. Sam had guessed. She remembered when she had her crush on

Andrew. That good feeling that hangs around you all the time, dreamy and happy. "I wouldn't call him a boyfriend, but yeah, he is pretty cool," Jenny said. "Let's not blab this to Mom and Dad, okay?"

"Sure," Sam said. She wanted to hear more, but she let it go.

"So you," Jenny asked again, "what are you up to?"

"I'm grounded," Sam sighed. "John, too."

"Really? You?" Jenny said. "You always do the right thing. How did you mess up?"

Sam poured out her story about Tracy, including giving her Jenny's friendship bracelet, but she didn't tell her about Sam's Secret Island. It felt good to talk to Jenny. She could talk to her like she talked to her friends, Abby and Sonya.

"I don't want vacation to end," Sam said.

"Yeah," Jenny agreed. "Well, you have until Sunday, don't you? Three more days anyway."

"Uh-huh, but only three days. You get to stay up here until the end of August," Sam said. She saw Jenny's face brighten. "You're lucky."

"We'll be back here next summer, I hope," Jenny said. "Your friend, Tracy, will be, too, I bet."

"Do you think you'll see this guy again? What's his name, Gus? That's a weird name," Sam asked. "How old is he?"

"Seventeen," Jenny answered.

"Does he have his driver's license?"

"Yeah," Jenny said.

"How many miles is it to Tacoma?"

"Stop!" Jenny said. Sam only stopped asking questions because Mom opened the back hatch of the van and loaded her bags of groceries.

"Where's your dad?" Mom asked. She glanced around the parking lot but got in the car to escape the rain. "Did Sam tell you that she and John met a friend this week?"

Mom asked. "They've spent all their time together. Even Chestnut has a buddy. Tracy has a little dog named Molly."

"She did tell me," Jenny said. "Sounds fun!"

"It was fun until yesterday," Sam said. She said the words under her breath and into the window of the car. A cloud of fog covered the glass and Sam started drawing on the window with her finger.

"Don't do that, honey, the windows get all dirty," Mom said, ignoring Sam's remark. Sam was ready to say something back to Mom, but she stopped when Dad opened the front door.

"We got it! Loganberry and marionberry," Dad said. He buckled up and looked at Mom. "You got the ice cream?"

Mom tilted her head at him as if to say, "Of course I got the ice cream."

"You're the best!"

John climbed in the back with a pie wrapped in foil and carefully set it on the seat between him and Sam.

"Who's up for a game of Monopoly?" Dad asked. "I feel lucky today."

"Can I build a fire in the fireplace?" John said. The idea of fire building cheered him up.

"Sure!" Dad answered. "Jenny?"

"The last time we played, I owned Park Avenue and Broadway and you ended up in jail, if I remember right!" she said.

"I'm going to win," Sam chimed in. "I'm going to buy everything I land on!"

✻ ✻ ✻

The rain never let up, but the afternoon went by quickly and Sam had to admit it was fun to be together. She almost won the Monopoly game, but her strategy of buying everything backfired when she landed in jail three times in a row. John won and Sam knew he wouldn't let anyone forget it for a long time.

They had an early dinner of Jenny's favorite mac and cheese, and John couldn't resist reminding Jenny for the millionth time how she had almost caught the kitchen on fire the first time she had tried to make it. Sam could see that Jenny loved the attention, and Sam guessed that, boyfriend or no boyfriend, Jenny missed her family a little.

After their delicious slices of pie, Sam went up to her room to do some drawing and Jenny followed.

"You're doing some cool stuff," Jenny said. She shuffled through a pile of drawings next to Sam's bed. "Maybe you'll be a famous artist."

"What are you going to be?" Sam asked.

"I don't know. This summer I discovered that I'm good with people." Jenny shrugged and jokingly opened her eyes wide. "Who knew?"

Sam thought about her sister's black clothes and eye makeup and being plugged into her earphones all the time. At first glance, it would be hard to believe that Jenny liked people. She could seem so distant and far away.

"I guess we can change," Sam said.

"For sure," Jenny said. "Look at you! You've changed a ton!"

"You think so? I mean, I feel different."

"Yeah," Jenny said. "Maybe the important changes are on the inside. Sort of that old 'don't judge a book by its cover' saying."

"Hmm," Sam replied.

"Girls!" Mom shouted up the stairs. "Time to go."

"So soon?" Sam asked Jenny.

"It's movie night and I don't want to miss it," Jenny said.

"Will Gus be there?" Sam teased.

Jenny threw a pillow at her sister. "Don't you dare say anything to Mom and Dad!" Jenny turned and went downstairs.

"You two want to stay here?" Mom said to Sam and John.

They looked at each other and nodded "yes."

"Just make sure you take Chestnut out for a bit," her mom said.

"And remember, you're grounded!" Dad said sternly.

"Give me a hug," Jenny said to Sam. "I'm gonna win Monopoly next time!" Jenny said to her brother, putting one arm around his shoulders. She knew John wasn't ever in the mood for a hug.

"Right," John scoffed. He looked at the floor and fidgeted.

Sam and John stood on the porch and watched them load into the van. The rain had stopped now and the clouds were thinning. The evening sun made the rain on the trees glow neon green, and a soft fog rose up from the woods as the rain evaporated.

They watched the van disappear onto the road.

"Let's take Chestnut for a walk," John said.

Sam looked at her brother. She knew what he was thinking and she agreed. What harm would it do to take a quick walk over to Sam's Secret Island? Chestnut needed the exercise and they had cabin fever.

"They'll be back in forty-five minutes," John said.

Sam ran in, grabbed the leash, hooked it onto Chestnut, walked to the trail at the end of the driveway, and turned in to the woods. The tall trees and short bushes were dripping with raindrops, but the last several times they had been on the trail, John had done a good job of breaking back the small branches that blocked their way. They escaped being soaked if they stuck to the trail.

"I wonder what Tracy is up to?" Sam asked.

"I don't know, probably in her room. Her dad was so mad!"

"What do you think Dad said to him?" Sam asked.

"I don't know. Dad doesn't like problems not to be solved. Maybe he calmed Tracy's dad down."

"Yeah," Sam said, "he's good at that."

They reached Sam's Secret Island, and John crawled under the tarp.

"Wow," he said. "This worked great. It's completely dry here! We could easily camp out in this spot."

"Fat chance we'll get to do that after yesterday," Sam said. She ducked down and stuck her head into the cave. There was no sign of a squirrel invasion, and her artwork still hung in its place. She saw Tracy's pictures of her mom were safe, and the snack container, too. "Looks good in here." Sam stood up. "Come on!"

She went back out to the main trail and turned towards Tracy's. She walked fast, dragging Chestnut, and John followed. They paused at John's trail marker and looked down to the beach. The tide was on its way out, and they could see the spot where they had found the big board and the rocky beach they had struggled to walk over. No wonder they had decided to swim! The evening sun was low on the horizon, and there was no wind on the water. It didn't look dangerous at all.

"Look," John said. He pointed to a piece of the bank that had broken off and slid to the beach. "The rain has made this even more slippery."

"You did a good job marking the spot," Sam said. "Let's go."

She took off and they came to the edge of the woods and walked a little ways into the field of fallen nettles. Sam stopped and stared at Tracy's house. The sunset glinted on the big windows, but the house looked empty and still. She thought of the lonely princess in the castle.

"Let's go back," John said.

"Look!" Sam said and pointed to the attic window. The window slid open and an arm appeared.

"Get down!" John said. "It might be the dad!" They fell flat on the ground, but in a moment they found the courage to take another look.

The window slid up and they could see Tracy. She leaned out and waved to them. Sam waved back, and as she did, Tracy threw something.

"Was that for us?" Sam asked.

"Only one way to find out," John said. He got up but stayed in a low hunch. "You stay here. I have my camouflage jacket on. You would be easy to see in that pink thing."

She looked at the sleeve of her pink poly-pro pullover and she had to agree.

John moved slowly across the nettle field to the gate and paused.

"Go along the fence!" Sam whispered this aloud to herself. Chestnut whined.

But John did the opposite of what Sam had wanted. He darted straight across the lawn to the side of the house and grabbed whatever had been thrown out the window. As he did so, the front door of the house slammed and John dove into the bushes along the house.

Sam heard a car engine start up and watched the SUV drive slowly down the driveway. She wondered who was driving. Maybe Grace Hardy, maybe Mr. Blakemore. Had Tracy been waiting for her and John to come to her? What was she doing in the attic? Perhaps her questions would be answered by whatever John had picked up.

John waited until the car reached the end of the driveway and then ran as fast as he could back to Sam.

"Come on," he said, barely stopping.

The two of them ran until Tracy's house was out of sight. They stopped and John handed Sam a wadded-up envelope.

He said nothing, bent over and gasping for breath with his hands on his knees.

"Better read as we go," he panted. "We have to beat Mom and Dad home!"

Sam opened the envelope as they walked down the trail. Inside was a handwritten note.

> *S & J,*
> *I am grounded! Tomorrow my dad is taking me to stay with friends in Bellevue. I hate him. I have to go to private school in the fall. PLEEZ STAY MY FRIENDS FOREVER.*
> *Bye for now, T & M*

When they reached Ravens Roost, Sam stopped. She felt the late sun on her shoulders and her wet toes inside her soggy tennis shoes. On her insides, she felt so sorry for her friend and so grateful for her own life.

Grateful for what, she couldn't quite say. It was something deep inside her, something made up of mac and cheese and Monopoly games, pesky little brothers, a mom and dad that cared too much, the coolest sister on the planet, and a slobbering dog.

And a friend named Tracy.

"We'll see her tomorrow," John said. "Come on!"

I don't think we will, Sam thought. *I don't think we will.*

From Sam's Secret Journal...

We made it back from Tracy's before Mom and Dad got home. Whew! John and I had to go to our rooms early as part of the being grounded thing. The rain has started up again. I hear it on the roof.

I wonder about Tracy.

In the note, she says she hates her dad. I don't think anybody should hate anybody. People have been mean to me before because of my Down syndrome, and it is hard not to be mean back. But I think hate is some kind of big misunderstanding.

I remember our first day on Orcas Island when I saw her all alone at the market. Seems like she is still alone, even if she has Molly.

We are leaving in three days. I hope we can see each other before I go. The way this is ending makes me sad.

Or is it the rain? I feel mixed up inside. Maybe I'll draw a picture.

More later...

CHAPTER 10

Runaway Girl

BANG, BANG, BANG!
Sam put down her sketchbook, leapt out of bed, and poked her head out her bedroom door. John stuck his head out of his room at exactly the same moment.

"That loud noise wasn't you?" Sam asked.

"Nope," John said. He walked down the hall, pausing at the top of the stairs and leaning down to listen. Sam came up behind him.

"Why are you stop—?"

John gestured for her to be quiet, and they crouched at the top of the stairs. Sam could see Dad's feet at the front door as he swung it open.

"Hey, Mark. What's up?" Dad asked. "Come in." A man's feet, muddy and wet, stepped onto the hall rug. Sam and John looked at each other and shrugged.

"Is she here?"

"Who is it, honey?" Mom asked from the living room.

"Mark Blakemore," Dad answered her. "You mean, Tracy?" he said to Mr. Blakemore. "No, we haven't seen her today. Like we talked about yesterday, we grounded the kids for not following directions."

"I don't know where she is! She's gone!" he said frantically.

"Take it easy, Mark. Come and sit down. Tell us what's going on," Dad said. He was using his best calm and confident doctor voice. It always made you feel more relaxed. Sam, Jenny, and John all agreed; it was like magic.

"Mom?" Sam called out. John jabbed her in the side. "Everything okay?"

In a flash, Mom came to the bottom of the stairs and looked up at them. Chestnut padded behind her and she looked up and whined.

"Nothing that concerns you two," Mom smiled a half smile. "Off to bed now."

The sound of the men's voices came from the living room.

"Is that Tracy's dad?" John asked.

"You two get up back upstairs," Mom said. "We're all going to bed right after this gets sorted out." She turned and opened the front door. "You go out for a second, Chestnut." Mom let the dog out and glanced back up at Sam and John. "Now!"

They went to their rooms and shut the doors, but in ten seconds they both peeked out again.

"Want to take a look?" John grinned.

He held out his trusty periscope and headed down the hall in his stocking feet. The two of them snuck down the stairs and quietly moved along the hallway to the entrance to the living room. John extended the periscope, took a look, and then handed it to Sam. She could see the backs of everyone's heads, and she also saw that it was Mr. Blakemore for sure. He was pacing up and down the small living room, red-faced and with his hands clenched. She wondered if he was always so stressed out.

"Tracy said she didn't want to go to a private school this fall!" Mr. Blakemore exclaimed. "But I didn't listen to her. I've been so afraid something would happen to her and now she has run off. This is my fault. Where could she have gone?"

Sam sucked in her breath and turned to John.

"Tracy's run away."

"Pretty hard to run away on an island," John whispered. Sam had to admit he had a point.

"Have you checked all over the house and the yard? Does she have other friends here?" Mom asked gently.

"She's not at home! I looked everywhere, and then I drove to town and the woods around the farmer's market. Now it's getting dark." He sat down on the couch and put his head in his hands. "If anything happens to her, I'll, I'll…."

Mr. Blakemore rubbed a big hand beneath his eye and stared at the floor. Sam could see how concerned he was, but it felt a little scary seeing a big man cry. She pulled in the periscope and stood back in the hall with John.

"Take it easy, Mark. How about you and I go drive around and take another look?" Dad suggested. "Did she have any money? She can't get off the island without taking the ferry. The last ferry leaves at 10:30 tonight."

"I don't know about any money. Let's just go." Mr. Blakemore jumped up to follow. "If we can't find her in the next hour, I'll call the police," he said.

John pointed back to the stairs. They crept up and went into his room and shut the door. John spun on his feet and looked at her.

"She must've been hiding in the attic when we saw her in the window," John said.

"Tracy didn't say anything in the note about hiding or leaving. Where would she go?" Sam asked. But as soon as she asked the question, she spoke the answer. "Sam's Secret Island!"

"We can't know that for sure," John said. "But we could go look. If she's not there, we don't have to give away our secret spot, and if she is..." John paused. "Well, I guess we'll be heroes."

John beamed a little. Sam knew he liked the idea of being a superhero and saving the day. He went over and grabbed his backpack and jacket from the hanging hooks on the wall, sat down on the edge of his bed, and put on his hiking boots.

"You go do the same," John said, picking up his backpack. "Get some shoes, turn the light out, and I'll meet you at the top of the stairs."

Sam did as she was told and grabbed her pink hoodie off the hook by her door as she left.

From the top of the stairs, Sam and John saw the front door open and Dad and Mr. Blakemore's feet walk out the door. They heard the crunch of steps on the gravel driveway and the doors of the van open and shut.

"Chestnut! Chestnut!" Mom called.

Chestnut usually came bounding back into the house after being let out for the last time at night. But tonight, Chestnut was nowhere to be seen. Mom mumbled something and they could hear her footsteps outside on the gravel driveway.

"Keep me posted!" she yelled to Dad. The van moved slowly down the driveway. Mom continued to call, but her voice faded.

"Chestnut, Chestnut!"

"I think she's gone around the corner of the house to the beach trail," John said.

Sam ran back to her bedroom and looked out her window across the yard of the cabin. In the twilight, she could make out Mom's shadow moving across the backyard. Sam hurried back to John.

"This is our chance; she's on the other side of the house!" Sam said.

And with that, they tiptoed down the stairs and out the front door. Outside, Sam ran to the edge of the driveway then continued on the dirt path so as not to make any noise with John right behind her.

Finally, they turned into the woods and started on the trail to Sam's Secret Island.

☆   ☆   ☆

"She's not here!" Sam yelled.

"What?" John asked. He came up behind Sam and set down his backpack.

The wind blew in the trees with a lonely whistle, and Sam felt a tingle run up her spine. It was a lot different to be in the woods at night.

"It's really getting dark now," Sam said. She folded her arms across her chest and hugged herself. She was glad to have her hoodie.

"Here," John said. He dug into his backpack and pulled out a big flashlight.

Leave it to her brother to save the day. For a quick moment, she believed that she had the best little brother in the universe.

"Let's go back into the cave and look around," John said.

Sam climbed after him across the big root and down into the cave. The tarp flapped and snapped outside in the breeze, but under the stump it was cozy on the dirt floor.

"No one home," John said. He cast the flashlight around the hideout.

"But look," Sam said. "My drawing is gone. And…" She stopped and bent over the opening under the stump where the snack box and Tracy's pictures were kept. "Tracy's pictures are gone. She's been here since this afternoon!"

"The question is, where is she now?" John asked. "We better go check the trail."

The rain fell harder now and the wind had picked up. Sam could hear the waves on the beach below and she really began to worry.

"It's Chestnut!" John yelled. The big dog stood in the flashlight beam, her pink tongue lolling out and her eyes brown pinpoints in the bright light. A muddy black Molly emerged between Chestnut's front paws.

"Oh my gosh," Sam said. "Molly, Molly, where is Tracy?"

Molly barked, turned, and ran with Chestnut close behind her. Sam and John chased the barking dogs until they came to a stop on the trail.

"Look!" John said.

In the beam of his flashlight was the trail sign he had built to mark the dangerous spot on the path. There was a new gash in the bank where another slice of dirt and brush had broken off and slid down. John cast the beam of light back and forth along the edge of the bank, and Sam spotted a piece of paper. She stooped and picked it up.

"It's my drawing," Sam said.

"Tracy?" John yelled. The dogs barked now, loud and continuously.

"Tracy?" Sam yelled, too.

John shined the flashlight along the steep slope, and this time the light caught the waving arm of their friend. She wasn't too far down the bluff. Tracy was half lying down, half sitting on a big bump of sandy dirt that had a few bushes growing on it.

"I'm here! I'm down here," she cried.

"Tracy! Tracy! We see you. We'll help you. Don't worry," John yelled.

"You go get help," Sam said to John. "I'll stay here with Tracy and Molly." She reached down and picked up the barking dog. "It's okay, Molly."

Molly stopped barking and gave Sam's cheek a lick.

"I'll take Chestnut. You keep this." John handed Sam the flashlight. "Be right back! Come on, girl," John said, and with that, he and Chestnut ran for help.

"John has gone to get help," Sam yelled down to her friend. Her eyes were adjusting to the early darkness, and now she could see Tracy without the flashlight. Sam sat down on the edge of the bluff and yelled down, "I have Molly. She's fine."

"I think I hurt my foot," Tracy said. "I'm afraid if I slide down to the bottom, I'll hurt it more."

At the sound of Tracy's voice, Molly gave a sharp bark and jumped out of Sam's arms. The dog scooted down the sandy slope and stopped where Tracy sat and wagged and nuzzled her owner.

"It's not that steep," Tracy said. "Molly did it. Do you think you could come down and we could get to the beach together? You don't have to, Sam. We can wait."

"I don't know," Sam said. She paused for a moment. She knew she could get flustered easily in a tense situation. But after watching Molly bound down the slope, she realized it wasn't all that steep. It certainly wasn't as steep as the rocky faces she practiced on every week at the Vertical Limit. "I'm going to try."

"Just go really slowly," Tracy said. "Head for me and it will be alright."

Sam stretched her legs out from her perch on the bank and very quickly she was taking broad steps in the sand. Her rock-climbing skills kicked in and she leaned in towards the bank to keep her balance and move carefully. In a moment, she was next to Tracy.

"Wow," Tracy said. "Good job!"

"I did it," Sam said.

As if in agreement, Molly gave Sam's cheek a lick. Sam felt her friend's tight grip on her arm, and she could feel her trembling. She pulled off her hoodie.

"Here," she said to Tracy. "Put this on. Together I think we can easily get to the bottom of the slope."

Tracy let go of Sam's arm and slipped on the pink jacket. Both girls looked down the sandy bank.

"Remember going on the slide when you were little?" Sam asked. "Well, that's what we're going to do, but you're going to be behind me riding piggyback. That way, if we go too fast, you won't land on your foot."

"Maybe I can hold the flashlight?" Tracy said.

Sam handed her the flashlight and scooted down in front of Tracy.

"This is good, both my hands are free," Sam said. Tracy got on piggyback style and put her arms around Sam's shoulders and her legs around her waist.

"Let's see where we're going," Tracy said, shining the flashlight down to the beach.

In the beams, they could see that they were still a fair ways above the beach, and luckily, the bank that had fallen before created a pile of dirt and sand that flattened out right at the beach above the driftwood. To the right was more of a drop off that ended in a pile of rocks. Sam hoped they could slide straight down and have a soft landing.

"Oh no," Tracy said. "Look, my mom's pictures." Tracy sobbed and shook.

Sam took the light and held it on the rocks at the bottom of the bank. There she could see twisted and broken picture frames and shards of broken glass. The photos were nowhere to be seen.

"It's okay, Tracy," Sam said. "We have to worry about getting down first. We'll find the pictures." She didn't know if this was true, but right now she would say anything to keep Tracy calm. "You have a job here. You're in charge of the flashlight, and you can't let go of me."

Tracy's crying hushed as she took the flashlight back from Sam.

"Alright," Sam said, "I'm going to try and keep us going slowly, but if we pick up speed, don't let go of me."

"Okay," Tracy sniffled. "What about Molly?"

"She'll be fine. She'll run beside us," Sam said. "Here we go."

Sam let up with her feet, and she was surprised how quickly she slid with the extra weight on her back. It seemed that if they leaned back, they would speed up, and she couldn't use her legs to dig in.

"Sit up straight," she said to Tracy.

She felt Tracy tighten her hold, and again Sam released her legs. They moved down the bank, but this time when she went to dig in her feet, the ground had turned to clay and her feet didn't grab. The two girls picked up speed.

"Hold on!" Sam yelled.

Tracy tightened her arms and legs around Sam and, in the process, dropped the flashlight. It bounced and rolled in front of them, throwing its light in all directions like a crazy light show.

The girls sped down the hill now. The flashlight landed to their right in the rocky area, and it seemed to Sam they were headed straight for it.

"Lean to the left!" she yelled. Sam tried to steer them, but they lost their balance and rolled once over each other before stopping on the flat pile of sand at the bottom of the bank.

For a moment, the two girls just lay there on their backs. The flashlight beam shone straight up into the sky, and the sound of the waves seemed peaceful after their wild ride.

"You okay, Sam?" Tracy asked. Molly came up to her and licked her face.

"Except for the sand in my mouth!" Sam said, spitting it out.

Tracy began to laugh.

"That was the craziest thing I've ever done! It was like sledding without snow."

"Not exactly what I had planned," Sam said. And then she started to laugh, too. She sat up and brushed off her face. "How is your foot?"

"Well, I'm not walking anyplace," Tracy said. "Any idea what the tide is doing?"

"If it's coming in, we'll be stuck here all night." Sam started laughing harder. "Do you think we can do *anything* on the beach and not get in trouble?"

"No," Tracy said. "I wouldn't want it any other way. Would you?"

The girls heard the dogs barking down the beach. John, Dad, and Mr. Blakemore emerged from the darkness into the glow of the flashlight.

"Sam!" Dad called.

"We're over here! We're fine, I mean. Tracy's foot is messed up," she answered.

Dad climbed up onto the pile of sand and shined his flashlight at Sam. He took off his sweater and handed it to her. She pulled it on and felt safe and relieved that she didn't have to be in charge anymore.

"Good job, Sam," Dad said. He bent down and gave her a quick kiss on the top of her head.

"Really, Dad, I'm good. Check out Tracy."

Mr. Blakemore showed up behind him.

"Tracy, Tracy," he said. "You gave me such a scare!" He fell to his knees and clutched his daughter in a bear hug. He looked angrily at Sam.

"Dad," Tracy said before he could say anything. "Sam saved me. She figured out a way and got us down the cliff. She's the hero."

Mr. Blakemore turned to Sam. His face softened.

"Thanks," he said and glanced to John. "Thanks to the both of you!"

"My pictures," Tracy said.

She pointed to John's flashlight, and they could all see the broken glass and picture frames. Her dad looked back to her.

"What pictures, honey?"

"Pictures of Mom," she said softly. "You took them all away. You put everything away. I know you didn't want to be reminded of her. Even me, I look too much like her. Now you want to put me away, too." Tracy buried her face in her dad's neck and began to sob again.

"Oh no! Never!" He hugged her tighter, rocking back and forth. "I just wanted to take care of the only thing I have left. The only person I have left that I love. You, my dearest girl, you."

"Let me check out that foot," Dad interrupted. He bent over Tracy and gently probed her leg and ankle. "Looks like a bad sprain. I think your dad is going to have to give you a piggyback ride home!"

"We can come and look for the pictures tomorrow," Mr. Blakemore said. "If we can't find them then we can find some new ones to put up. Does that sound like a plan?"

"Thank you, Dad," Tracy said.

"Okay, let's get you loaded up here," he said. "We ready to go, everyone?"

John ran and grabbed the flashlight, and Dad helped Sam get up. The wind had died down and the clouds had thinned. The moon shone in the sky, with wisps of clouds across its face lighting up their path down the beach.

"Follow me," John called out.

"Hold on, Tracy," her dad said and swung her up on his back.

"Second piggyback ride I've had today!" Tracy yelled. She looked over her shoulder at Sam. "The first one was the most fun."

Sam laughed at her friend. Dad took her hand, and they walked home in the moonlight.

From Sam's Secret Journal...

It has been two weeks since we came home from our vacation at Ravens Roost, and today we are up early to go back to Orcas Island and get Jenny from camp. The best part is that I'm going to see Tracy before we go home later today. Mom and Dad are going to drop John and me off while they pick up Jenny.

It seems like a million years since our big adventure on the bluff. Tracy ended up in the ER and she had a bad sprain just like Dad said. We went with Mom and Dad to her house the next day and we all got a chance to explain our side of the story.

Here in town, it's been hot and stuffy and I miss the sounds of the beach and woods, but it's great to see Abby and Sonja. All they want to do is talk about school shopping and who they hope will be in their homeroom classes this year.

They tell me that I look different. I don't think I look different, but I know I feel different. My Seattle friends are seeing what I feel. Wow, that's impossible to explain!

As much I don't like math, the idea of school is always kind of exciting by the end of August. I'm wearing a new pair of shoes and jeans that I bought for school. The shoes are short leather boots. Can't wait to show them to Tracy!

CHAPTER 11

Goodbye

The van pulled off the ferry and Sam watched the tall trees alongside the road zoom by. In the breaks between trees, she could see fields that were no longer green, but a dried-out yellow. The exhaust from the long line of cars off the ferry tossed and blew the roadside flowers, whose droopy heads seemed to say, "We're tired."

"Quick, stop at the farmers market," Dad announced.

"Dad!" Sam said. She was inpatient to see Tracy. She looked at her new boots. She was wearing them with a new pair of jeans and felt really happy with her outfit. She was dying to show Tracy.

"Last chance for pie. Apple season is here," he said wistfully.

Mom chuckled and shook her head. "The only thing missing in our relationship is my ability to make pie," she said and looked out the window. "I wonder if it's genetic?"

Sam smiled at Mom. It was true; she could do everything but make a pie. Dad reached across and grabbed her hand.

"I love you anyway," he said and laughed.

Sam glanced at John, who shrugged his shoulders. He hated romantic stuff.

Sam read a big sign at the end of the turn off for the market:

"Last Saturday Market, September 2nd"

September 2nd! That was next weekend, and school started the following Tuesday. Where had the summer gone?

They parked and piled out of the car to stretch their legs, and Dad dashed off to the pie booth. Sam put Chestnut on her leash. When Jenny got home, Sam wouldn't be in charge of Chestnut anymore. She scratched the big dog behind the ears. She and Chestnut had enjoyed a lot of freedom this summer, and Jenny kept Chestnut on a pretty short leash. Sam would remember to tell her sister that Chestnut really loved a chance to run free.

Dad returned quickly, carrying a pie wrapped in foil with two outstretched hands, as if it was a royal crown on a velvet pillow.

"Gravensteins!" he said.

"Frankensteins?" John asked.

"Apples!" Dad replied.

Sam rolled her eyes at John, and he shot her a look and gently kicked her.

"Mom, John just kicked my boots!"

"John!" Mom said.

Sam figured that John was still getting back at all of them for their recent school shopping expedition. John absolutely didn't care about school clothes. In fact, when they went shopping—which Sam decided she would never,

never in a million years do with her brother ever again—he refused to buy anything but new underwear.

"I like my old backpack," he said. John had clutched at it as though it was incredibly valuable. He didn't want to give up his camo jacket either, even though by the end of the summer, the zipper was broken and one of the pockets was ripped. "It has the perfect number of pockets!" he explained. He had stood hunched in the jacket, like a turtle pulling into the safety of a shell, and looked at Mom with a scowl. Mom ignored him.

"Try this one."

She'd held up a sleek poly-pro jacket. It was royal blue with a logo of something across the back.

"No way!" John said. He wore an expression that reminded Sam of the time they had to give their cat a bath. A wet cat had a certain look.

But the most embarrassing part of the shopping expedition was, when he finally did make a decision and get excited about something, it was all about new underwear with superheroes on the front. Sam thought she was going to die when they were in the checkout line, and she had excused herself and gone over to a magazine rack and buried herself in a magazine.

Brothers, she thought. *Some things never change!*

This afternoon at Jenny's camp, there was a lunch for the campers and their families. There would be an awards ceremony, and camp counselors and staff would be honored and teased in fun skits created by the campers. Sam had begged Mom and Dad to let her see Tracy instead, and they had finally agreed if John could go along with her.

Sam's first thought was that it was completely unfair, but as she thought about it, her summer vacation had included John in big ways. She had to admit he was a lot of fun when he was doing his goofy spy thing.

The van turned off the main road to the lane to Ravens Roost and Tracy's house.

"New renters at the cabin," Mom commented.

Dad drove slowly by the end of the driveway to the cabin. Sam craned her neck to see if she could get a glimpse of the new renters. She saw a girl who was younger than her and a baby who was sitting on the grass next to one of the garden gnomes. How strange it seemed that other people could stay at their cabin. Their time was over; now it was someone else's turn.

The van swung into the Blakemores' long driveway, and before they were halfway up, Tracy appeared on the front porch, jumping up and down with Molly in her arms. The van slowed and stopped, and Sam, John, and Chestnut spilled out. Mr. Blakemore appeared behind Tracy, looking more relaxed than Sam had ever seen him, and extended his hand to Dad and Mom. Grace Hardy came up behind him, laughing and giving everyone hugs.

"Sam and John are so looking forward to this visit," Mom said to Mr. Blakemore. "We have to get over to Jenny's end-of-camp party."

"Sure, I understand," he nodded and smiled. "We're so happy to see our friends again. We're going back to Bellevue tomorrow. We've rented a house in our old neighborhood, and Tracy is going back to her old school."

"I'm going into town to help with Tracy," Grace added. "I'll come up on weekends, for now, to visit Dan. I think he likes the idea of being on his own up here!" And as usual, Grace laughed.

Sam stood next to Tracy and noticed her hair. She had a bleached, light pink stripe in her hair right behind her ear. Sam stared in envy.

"Let's go upstairs," Tracy said to Sam and John.

"We'll be back in a couple hours," Dad called after them. "We're shooting for the 5:00 p.m. ferry!"

Sam heard the grown ups' voices saying their goodbyes as she followed Tracy up the big stairs to her bedroom. The landing at the top of the stairs had changed. Photos of Tracy with both her mom and dad and pictures of all of them as little kids gave the walls of the landing and the hallway a happy feeling. No longer were there any mystery shadows and blank spots on the walls.

Before John could ask to play Xbox, Tracy just pointed in the direction of the big-screen TV and nodded at him.

"Thanks!" John said. He walked over, picked up a controller, and sat down. Molly trotted behind him and curled up on the rug next to him. He reached down and scratched her back.

"Let's go," Tracy whispered to Sam.

They two girls quietly left the bedroom, and Sam followed Tracy into the library. Tracy didn't bother with the hidden key but walked straight to the stairs and motioned for Sam to follow her. Sam was surprised when they reached the attic to see that most of the furniture and boxes were gone.

"This looks different," Sam said. "Where is all the stuff?"

"Well, Dad and I decided that we would go through my mom's things together. At first I thought it would be too hard, and I think he did, too." Tracy paused. "You remember that time you told me that guys just want to seem strong?" Sam thought about Dad and John and nodded at Tracy. "I guess dads have feelings like everybody else. I mean, they're strong, too."

"I guess you can be strong and have lots of feelings at the same time," Sam said. She was thinking about the time a big kid had bullied her at the bus stop. It turned out he wasn't as mean and tough as he had seemed. In fact, Sam thought he was kind of lonely.

"Anyway," Tracy continued, "we made a deal that we would choose only the most important things from our old life with Mom in Bellevue and that we would combine that with new things for our new life. Dad has changed some work plans so that he can be home more, and I still have Grace for the time being. Next year, he might open a new office in Bellevue, or we might live in India for a year."

"Wow," Sam said. "You guys have figured out a lot of stuff." Sam tried to remember what she knew about India. In her mind's eye, she saw elephants and cows in the streets, but she knew it was a modern country, too. Once she had seen a booth at a fair that offered Indian henna tattoos in all kinds of intricate designs. Mom wouldn't let Jenny get one.

"What about you?" Tracy asked. "I love your jeans and boots!"

"You do?" Sam said. "Abby and Sonja talked me into them. It was good to see my friends again. They're shop-o-holics!"

"I had a sleepover last week with my friend, Susan, in Bellevue," Tracy said. "Our new place will be near her. We went school shopping and we got our hair done. What do you think?" Tracy held her hair up at the back of her head and Sam could see the light pink hair around the base of her neck.

"That is way cool," Sam said.

"I talked Dad into it because when my hair is down, you really can't see it," she said. Tracy dropped her hair down and shook her head. Sam could still see strands of the light pink sticking out.

"Hmm," Sam said. "I don't think that would work on my mom!" Sam had sat down on an old sofa. "So maybe you won't be back here next year?" she asked.

"Maybe not," Tracy said.

"That sucks," Sam said. Mom hated it when anyone used that word, but Mom wasn't there and it described exactly how she felt.

The two girls were quiet.

"Hey!" Tracy piped up. "Let's go to Sam's Secret Island, for old time's sake."

"Should we tell John?" Sam asked.

"No, just you and me! Come on!"

With that, she leapt up, and the girls ran down the attic stairs and then down the big stairs. Mr. Blakemore and Grace were nowhere to be seen as Tracy slipped into her sneakers by the front door. The girls hurried out the door and around the side of the house. It was late afternoon now, and the sun shone at an angle across the lawn that gave the yard a golden glow. They went through the gate, and a cool breeze picked up as they got closer to the bank above the beach. Sam could feel the new season making its way into the days of summer.

"My dad cleared the brush off of the steps. He really loves going down to the beach now. Your dad inspired him to take up kayaking," Tracy said.

They stopped at the top of Tracy's steps and looked down the stairs. Sure enough, at the bottom landing, Sam could see a bright yellow kayak tethered to the railing. She turned and followed Tracy across the field and into the woods. They walked quickly along the trail to the hideaway. Sam glanced down at her new boots. They weren't as comfortable as her summer tennis shoes and she was worried they would get muddy, but the trail was dry and the sounds of her steps were hollow and soft on the compact trail of dirt, pine needles, and leaves.

Sam was first onto the trail to the hideaway. The stump looked smaller to her, and John's tarp had come untied and hung listlessly on the ground, which was covered with fallen leaves. Sam decided not to crawl into the cave and get her new school clothes dirty. She stopped and looked around, and Tracy stopped next to her.

"I've come here a few times to sit and think," Tracy said. "I didn't tell my dad about it."

"So, Sam's Secret Island is still a secret?" Sam said.

"Yeah," Tracy said.

Somehow this made Sam feel better about the end of summer. Before she could say anything else, the squirrel popped up onto the top of the stump and chattered them.

"Oh my gosh," Tracy said. She turned and ran back out the trail with Sam right behind her. They stopped at the main trail and turned to look. The squirrel's scolding was even louder now, and his whole body shook and twitched from his perch on the dead tree stump.

"Wow, I guess it's his hideaway now," Sam said. She was laughing and out of breath.

"Until next summer anyway," Tracy said. "It's 'Squirrel's Secret Island'!"

"Bye, squirrel," Sam yelled. "Take good care of everything!" And they turned and walked back towards Tracy's.

Tracy led the way now, and she walked right by the place on the bluff where she had slipped. Sam stopped, stood, and looked down. Even more of the bank had slid away since Tracy's accident. She wondered what it would be like by the time they came back next year.

If we come back next year, she thought.

"Here's the bluff!" Sam called and Tracy walked back to her. "I'm sorry you had that accident."

"I'm not," Tracy said. Sam looked at her in surprise. "Nothing would have changed for the better for me and Dad. I don't know how it would have been without that night, but maybe we would have been unhappy longer, or grown apart even more. It seemed like a bad thing, but it was really a good thing. Do you think that's possible?"

Sam paused and thought. She knew a lot about things being part good and part bad. Her Down syndrome was the big example for her. In her heart, she knew that it was a hard thing and that it made her different, but in her heart she also knew that it didn't matter. She was good at some things and not so good at other things, just like everyone else. Most important, she knew she had people who loved her, and now she had a new friend. A new school year was ahead of her and it would have its ups and downs, but she had just had the best vacation of her life.

"For sure it's possible," Sam answered. "Most definitely."

As she said that, the bushes rustled and Molly burst out. The little dog ran to Tracy, who swooped her up in a big hug. Molly turned in Tracy's arms and barked at the bushes. Sam caught sight of the top of John's periscope, and she silently pointed it out to Tracy. Tracy nodded her head when she saw it.

"Hey, Sam, you sure have a crazy little brother!" Tracy said loudly.

The periscope lurched and John stood up with a faked hurt expression on his face and made his way noisily through the bushes. "I'm not crazy!" he said. He was wearing his old camo jacket and carrying his spy backpack. "You two are the crazy ones. Girls!"

Sam and Tracy looked at each other and laughed, and Molly wiggled and wagged.

Some things never change, Sam thought.

And with that, the summer friends walked home.

Made in the USA
Middletown, DE
03 December 2017